This story is a work of fiction. Names, characters and incidents are fictitious. Any similarities to actual persons, locations, or events is coincidental.

ISBN: 978-1-989206-74-4

Camp Neverland Copyright © 2021 UNNERVING
Camp Neverland Copyright © 2021 Lisa Quigley

UNNERVING

"*Camp Neverland* offers a spellbinding atmosphere of folklore, friendship, and murder that feels too good to be true, and yet thanks to Quigley's sinister magic, we want to belong all the more. An engrossing coming-of-age journey into the heart of loneliness and sacrifice."
 – Hailey Piper, author of *The Worm and His Kings*

"Quigley's camp nightmare will keep you up all summer—a deliciously dark coming-of-age campfire story that is both modern and timeless."
 – Scott Thomas, author of Kill Creek and Violet

# CAMP NEVERLAND

LISA QUIGLEY

For Sara, Leah, Ty, Mackenzie, Angel, and Danielle. Because you're the best women I know, and because you accept me completely. (And you've never asked me to kill anyone. At least, that's the story I'm sticking to...)

# PART ONE: INK

# CHAPTER ONE

Max Grayson got her first period at sixteen years old in the middle of a school day and had basically bled out in front of the entire school. Max hadn't even had the chance to discover it. When the bell rang and everyone stood up, the whole class figured it out for her due to the huge red stain on the seat of her jeans. And because Murphy's Law and all that, it was the one class she shared with Chuck Snyder, who'd had it out for her since the second grade. If anyone had managed to miss the stain, Chuck announced it loudly enough to fix that for them. And of course, the whole fiasco gave her a new nickname. It wasn't long after that all the strange things started happening with her drawings.

But Max didn't need to worry about any of that for the rest of the summer.

She watched the landscape slide past outside the car window, having shifted from industrial buildings and residential homes to mountain inclines covered in bright green pine trees hours ago. The Vermont sky was a blue so bright it almost looked fake, like something out of a story book. A lone hawk flew over the two-lane highway. Max caressed the worn Camp Neverland pamphlet with damp hands and exhaled a slow, shaky breath. The usual tightness in her chest had eased some; the farther away they got from home the better.

"Excited?" Her mom risked a quick glance away

from the road.

Max shrugged. "I guess."

"Lot of money for 'I **guess**,'" her mom said, eyes refocused ahead, lips tightened.

"All right, sure," Max said, "I am." It's not that she *wasn't* excited. The pamphlet promised a lot of things, and Max worried she'd arrive to discover it was all too good to be true.

"I had to press your dad for the extra funds," her mom continued. "And you know how his wife *hates* that."

Max knew all of this already. Every single one of her parent figures had made sure of it. She sighed.

"Max?" her mom's voice softened. "You know you don't have to go? This was your idea."

"I want to." Max looked at her mom and shaped her face into a pleading look she hoped was enough to appease her. It worked for now. An awkward silence settled inside the car.

Max looked back outside, eyes basking in all the lush green. She rolled down her window and breathed in the sharp scent of pine. The wind tousled her already unruly hair and Max tucked an errant red curl behind her ear. She caught the reflection of her hazel eyes in the side mirror, cautious and hopeful and deep-set in pale, freckled skin. The green landscape roared past.

Max wouldn't have even known about the camp if the pamphlet hadn't arrived in the mail, addressed specifically to her. *Maxine Grayson.* It was rare she got her own mail. It hadn't arrived by carrier owl and it wasn't her ticket to some secret school of witchcraft, but it had still felt personal, somehow, like her own private invitation to escape the drudgery of her real life.

But camp wasn't cheap. Max knew her mom had heaped extra guilt tactics onto her dad for his contribution to the funds, and she didn't even feel bad about it. She never asked for anything.

The pamphlet had promised stories told around campfires under a night sky filled with endless stars and days filled with artistic endeavors. It promised a a summer away from the dramas of high school, tucked deep in the lush green mountains of Vermont. Reading and drawing and swimming and hiking would be a dream come true for Max.

And *even if* Camp Neverland was too good to be true, Max was certain of at least one thing: she'd have nearly an entire summer without the anxiety of possibly running into Chuck Snyder. That alone was worth the risk of a few dashed hopes.

The car slowed. Max's mother turned off onto a side road that veered right into the wooded green mountains. Max's heart leapt and wiped her palms on her jeans.

The thick green forest was alive with the sounds of singing birds and chirping insects, loud through the car's open window. Max lost herself in the twists and bumps of those dirt back roads and before she knew it, her mom was slowing to a stop in front of a rusty gate, opened wide in preparation of incoming campers. Above the fence was a huge worn wooden sign, *Camp*

*Neverland* sprawled across it in bold white lettering. The car rolled through the gateway.

# CHAPTER TWO

Max's mom stopped the car in front of what appeared to be the main building. A small sign that said CAMP PRE-REGISTRATION was on the front door.

"It looks awfully run down." Her mom eyed the building.

The buildings were old, the wood splintered and weather-worn, but the area was clean and the grounds well-kempt. "It's remote. Not run down." Max shrugged. "There's a difference."

"I don't know..." Her mom swiveled around in her seat. "What do we really know about this place?"

"*Mom.*" Max groaned. "Seriously? You called and spoke with someone, right? It's an old camp in the middle of the woods. It's *supposed* to be rustic. That's the *point.*"

Her mom sighed. "Yeah. Yes, you're right. Sorry. I just want you to be safe."

"I'm sixteen. I'll be fine."

A loud rap on Max's window made them both jump.

A girl with disconcertingly pale skin and nearly translucent blue eyes stood outside the car. Her straight blond hair grazed her hip bones. She wore cut-off jean shorts and a striped tank top. She met Max's eyes with a gaze so intense it was uncomfortable.

"Hello," she said. "Sorry if I scared you. I was just excited to introduce myself. I'm Tanya. One of the senior campers? You must be Max."

Max's cheeks warmed beneath the inquisitive stare of Tanya's lucid blue eyes. "How'd you know?"

Tanya smiled. "I've been coming to Camp Neverland for years. It's quite selective. We're so happy you'll be joining us."

"Oh," Max said. She was never *chosen* for anything, always chosen last for team sports. 'Chosen last'—a generous expression. When you're 'chosen last,' you're not *chosen* at all. It just means some unlucky team gets stuck with you after they're done *choosing* everyone else.

"Do you know where I'll find a—?" Max's mom glanced at the piece of paper she'd dug out of her purse. "Miss Judy Florence?"

"Miss Flo?" Tanya gestured toward the door at the front of the main building. "She's the Head Mistress. Inside at the registration desk."

"Thanks." Max's mom's lips thinned into what was supposed to be a smile. "Hun, did you want to come in with me, or..."

"Why don't you stay with me?" Tanya said. "I'll show you around, take you to our cabin."

"Go." Max waved at her mom. "I'm fine."

Just then, Ms. Grayson flinched. She squeezed her eyes shut and pinched the bridge of her nose between two fingers.

"Mom?" Max said.

"A headache," Ms. Grayson muttered. "All that driving."

"You still have to drive back," Max said, worried.

"I'll be fine," her mom said. "Just need a little water."

"You'll find some inside," Tanya said, features smooth and placid.

Ms. Grayson nodded. "Thanks. Meet back at the car in ten?"

"Yeah." Max glanced at Tanya, whose smile was alluring and mysterious.

The screen door snapped shut behind Ms. Grayson, who disappeared inside. Max stepped out of the car and reached for her backpack, heavy with her favorite comics. The usual suspects were all in there: *Sandman*, *Lucifer*, *Locke and Key*. But her absolute favorite was *Black Magic* because it was illustrated by a woman: Nicola Scott. She slung one strap around her shoulder and turned to face Tanya.

"That all you brought?"

Max blushed. "No, I have a duffle bag."

"Let me." Tanya headed to the car.

"Oh, you don't have to—"

"I insist."

"Oh, well, okay," Max said. "It's in the trunk."

Tanya hit the silver button to pop the trunk. She grabbed the strap of Max's deep green duffle bag and slung it over her shoulder. She tucked a strand of silvery blonde hair behind her ear and that's when Max saw the tattoo on the inside of Tanya's wrist: a snake curled into the shape of a figure eight. When she straightened up, she caught Max staring at it. Tanya winked.

"Come on," Tanya said. "I'll show you to your bunk."

Max followed behind Tanya on the worn dirt path. They passed clusters of smiling, chattering girls who waved and smiled. The soft dirt puffed up in little clouds beneath their sneakers and the warm summer air buzzed with insects.

Men in khaki ranger-style uniforms tended the grounds, their go-carts loaded with rakes and shovels of varying sizes. One of them caught Max's eye and smiled broadly, his mouth closed.

Max smiled back tentatively, then inhaled a deep breath of sweet summer aromas. Turned earth and fresh-cut grass and sweet violets and honeysuckle and pine. The air felt different there in these green mountains, more honest. Max had never been anywhere that felt so *friendly*. Bees buzzed, insects hummed, birds chirped. She inhaled deeply of the rich pine scent again and thought she might never leave Vermont.

Tanya looked back and caught the look on Max's face. "Gorgeous, right?" she said. "Makes you want to stay forever."

"How do you do that?" Max blurted.

"Do what?" Tanya turned back to the trail.

What Max really wanted to say was *read my mind*, but instead she went with, "It's like you know me or something." She immediately regretted her words. It seemed too intimate a thing to say.

Tanya shrugged. "I don't have to *know* you," she said. "We're all alike, here."

"How so?"

"It's simple," Tanya said. "Camp Neverland attracts...a certain type of person."

Max slowed. What if she wasn't the right kind of person for Camp Neverland?

"Don't worry," Tanya said. "You'll fit right in."

Max smiled. "Did it again."

"What?"

"You read minds?"

"I'm psychic." Tanya's laugh was musical. "Also, we've all been where you are."

Max thought about the sketchbooks in her backpack, filled with stylized drawings of kids from school and suspected that wasn't *quite* true. "Where's that?"

"Just looking to belong." Tanya stopped in front of a small building and turned around. Her silvery blue eyes locked onto Max's. "Home sweet home."

Max eyed the wooden placard with worn lettering above the door. *Cabin 13.*

"Before you go spouting off some rhetoric about 'thirteen' being unlucky or whatever, please understand that is complete and utter misogynistic garbage," she said. Her voice sparkled with mirth.

"It is?" Max's dad had a thing about the number. He would never take an elevator that stopped on the thirteenth floor, he always skipped the thirteenth stair, typical stuff like that.

"It's a sacred number." Tanya looked at the placard above the door with reverence. "Holy. The number of the goddess."

Max lifted an eyebrow. "Really? Never heard that."

Tanya rolled her eyes. "Of course not. The patriarchy demonized everything beautiful, anything that gave women power."

"Yeah," Max said, not fully understanding but instinctively wanting to cheer anyway. She was thinking of Nicola Scott's subversive art in *Black Magic* and how boys talked about female comic book artists online.

"Anyway," Tanya said, "Cabin Thirteen is the final cabin on the girl's side, and it's the *luckiest* of them all."

She pushed the screen door open and Max noticed that its only lock was a small silver hook and loop. "Couldn't anyone just break in?"

Tanya grinned. "We don't worry about that here."

Max brushed a red curl from her eyes. She felt more relaxed and at ease than she had since...well, ever. She swallowed another deep gulp of crisp mountain air and told herself not to get her hopes up too high, but it was far too late for that.

The cabin's interior was long and narrow and sparsely furnished. The wooden floor planks were worn, but clean of dirt and dust. The walls were exposed wood. Beds lined the walls, but they weren't traditional double bunks. The beds were high up, but instead of a second bed underneath, there were simple wooden desks.

Each bunk had its own long window. The windowpanes were thrust wide open, so the warm mountain air filled the room through the screens. The sweet summer sounds of the breeze in the trees outside and the soft hum of insects drifted in.

"Like it?" Tanya said, eyeing Max.

Max grinned. "It's perfect."

Tanya led Max to a bare bunk in the corner. "This one's yours," she said. "Welcome home."

*Home.* Max avoided Tanya's eyes, afraid they would betray the way her heart was bursting open. She plunked her backpack on the bare top bunk mattress.

"You brought a sleeping bag and pillow?"

Max nodded. "In the car."

"Good," Tanya said. "We'll get you settled. It will be dinner soon and we'll meet the other girls at the mess hall."

They stepped out the cabin door and onto the dirt path.

"Thanks," Max said. "You've been so helpful."

"Of course," Tanya said. "We wanted you in our cabin. You're special, Max."

Being wanted—*chosen!*—was a new experience. Max reeled inside and watched her feet move steadily along the dirt path.

The pamphlet had been right about this place. She savored the sensation of wonder.

On the way back to the car, Tanya gestured toward the cluster of numbered cabins that surrounded their own. "This is the girl's side," she said.

"And the boy's?" Max said. She would have much preferred a summer getaway without the threat of boys.

But the pamphlet had been *very* clear that Camp Neverland was a safe and inclusive place.

"Other side of the lake," Tanya said.

Max swiveled her head around. She hadn't noticed a lake.

Tanya grinned. "I'll show you. There's a trail through the forest." She pointed at a large barn-like structure a short way away. "That's the mess hall. And over there, that cluster of buildings? That's the art center. That's where many of the daily activities take place. But you'll get the full tour tomorrow."

Max's mom was waiting when they arrived back at the car, a worried crease between her brows. "All paid up."

Max smiled. "Good."

Ms. Grayson's mouth twisted. She glanced at Tanya. "I guess...that's it?"

Max shrugged. "Yeah."

"Do you...need help getting the rest of your things?"

"Um, I don't think so," she said. "It's just my bedding. And—"

"We've got it from here, Mrs. Grayson," Tanya said.

"*Ms.* Grayson," Max's mom corrected. "Just Ms. now."

Max rolled her eyes. Her mom hadn't changed her last name after the divorce, but she was very sensitive about ensuring everyone knew she wasn't married anymore.

"So sorry," Tanya said, her face erupting with a warm smile. "Ms. Grayson. Please, don't worry. We'll take care of your girl."

Ms. Grayson offered a tight smile. "I certainly hope so."

She guided Max toward the car and leaned in so their eyes were level. "Honey," she said, "you sure about this?"

Max groaned. "Of course."

"But you're *sure*?"

"Mom." Max made a sound in the back of her throat. "What's your deal?"

Her mom looked over her shoulder at Tanya, who was standing back to give them privacy but smiling sweetly.

"This place gives me the creeps." Ms. Grayson closed her eyes and rubbed her temples.

"Headache still?" Max said.

"Something isn't right," her mom said. "Ever since we got here, I feel dizzy, and my head aches. A little nauseous, too."

"We were in the car for hours," Max said. "Did you get water?"

"I did." Her mom blinked several times. "I just feel so strange. I was totally fine until we pulled up."

Max wanted to be sympathetic, but she resented having to dampen her excitement. "Why are you ruining this for me?"

"Honey, I'm not—"

"Can't you let me have one thing?" Max said. "Just one."

"Maxine." Her mother's voice hardened. "Stop it.

You're being ridiculous. I'm not *taking* anything from you."

"As usual, it's all about you," Max said.

"It's not, I'm not—" Ms. Grayson winced and squeezed the bridge of her nose with two fingers again. "I just want you to be safe."

"I'll be fine," Max said.

Ms. Grayson nodded. "Miss Flo was—um, **exceptionally nice.**" She stopped then, wavered slightly. She placed a hand on the car to steady herself. "It just— it seemed odd."

"Odd to be nice?"

Ms. Grayson shrugged. "No. I don't know." She sighed deeply. "I'm sorry. You're right. Maybe I'm just used to—"

"People being dicks? Me too."

"Maxine! Language!"

Max shrugged. She'd gotten two '*Maxines*' in less than a minute, some kind of record. "Sorry."

"I really don't feel well," Ms. Grayson said. "It's so hard to focus. Do you feel okay?"

"I'm fine," Max said. "Do you need to lay down or something?"

A perceptible shudder passed through her mom. "No, I—I need to *go*. I need to, um, they want me to...I'm sorry, honey. What were you saying?"

"Mom," Max said. "You're freaking me out."

"Okay, sweetie, well if you're sure, then I guess I'll go."

Something wasn't right, but Max didn't want to deal

with it. "I'm sure," Max said.

Her mom held up her baby finger. She wavered as though drunk. "Pinky promise?"

Max rolled her eyes but looped her own pinky into her mother's. It was something they'd done forever and the action was comforting. "Pinky promise."

"Okay." Ms. Grayson shook her head a few times, like trying to clear it. "*Okay.*"

Max waved at Tanya, who glided over to the car. "All set?" Tanya said.

Max squealed. Tanya helped her collect her bedding.

Ms. Grayson hugged Max tightly. "I'll miss you," she whispered into Max's red curls.

Max nodded. "You too."

Ms. Grayson climbed into the car and slammed the front door shut. She poked her head from the window, looking back one last time. "I love you."

"Be careful, okay?" Max said.

Her mom titled her head quizzically. "You know what's weird?" She turned the car on. "I already feel better. Huh. Must have just been dehydrated."

Max's brow furrowed. "Okay, if you're...sure."

But the car was already rolling forward. "Have a great summer, sweetheart!" Her mom waved her hand out of the window.

Max's heart fluttered in her chest as she watched her mom's car disappear down the driveway. One part of herself wanted to break into a run on the dirt road, climb back into the car, make sure her mom got home safely, forget about this whole thing. That small part of herself whispered, *Run.*

But Max forced her eyes away from the car's taillights. This summer was about *her.* She shushed that small, quiet, timid voice.

She chose to heed the louder voice inside, instead. The one that screamed, *Stay.*

# CHAPTER THREE

The mess hall hummed with excited chatter, the tables already filling up with lively boys and girls. Max paused in the doorway behind Tanya. Tanya made Max feel wanted, but she was just one person. Max might not get so lucky with everyone else.

Tanya, a few steps ahead, turned around. "Coming?"

"I'm…"

Tanya touched Max's shoulder, gently. "Everyone's really nice."

Max exhaled and hadn't even realized she'd been holding her breath. "Yeah. Okay. Thanks. Sorry."

"For?"

"Um." Max laughed shakily. "I don't really know."

"Exactly." Tanya grinned. "Come on. Let's get some grub and meet the others."

Max followed Tanya through the cafeteria line. Max was used to unappetizing school lunches but the aromas here were tantalizing. Her mouth watered.

Tanya noted the look on Max's face. "The food is incredible," she said.

Max nodded. "It looks great."

Tanya mimed a chef's kiss. "All the vegetables are grown right here on the land."

They wound their way through the crowd to a table, where three other girls with their own full trays sat expectantly. Their faces glowed.

"Max," Tanya said, "meet Isabelle, Julia, and Violet."

The girl closest to the end of the table reached for Max's hand, and Max caught a glimpse of the snake tattoo on her inner wrist—the same figure eight shape as Tanya's. "I go by Izzy." She flashed a smile, teeth bright against dark skin. "So happy you're here."

Izzy scooched over and Tanya slid onto the bench. She patted the empty space next to her, and Max sat down.

Across from Max was a girl with straight brown hair and dark blue plastic glasses propped upon a nose sunburned pink, and a light-skinned girl with a short shock of purple hair.

"Um, Violet?" Max guessed.

The girl with purple hair and the angled jaw grinned. "Valiant guess," she said. "Sadly, I'm not that on the nose. Julia. But call me Jules."

"I'm Violet," the sunburned girl said, voice soft and gentle. Kind, wide brown eyes shined behind her glasses. "Did Tanya give you the grand tour?"

"Sort of," Max said. "I saw our cabin, anyway."

"You'll get the full treatment tomorrow," Jules said.

"Cool," Max said. She was about to ask how the art programs worked when there was a commotion at the mess hall entrance. Everyone at the table paused their conversation and turned their heads toward the noise.

A group of boys had burst in through the big double doors, laughing and speaking loudly. Their voices boomed and echoed through the space. One voice in particular cut through the air, taking all the breath from Max's lungs. She tried to shrink smaller in her seat.

Tanya's hand was on her shoulder. "Max, hon?" she said. "You look ill."

Max shook her head and tried, unsuccessfully, to make herself unnoticeable. It was too late, anyway, because Chuck Snyder had already seen her. He always had a way of finding her in any crowd.

"What do we have here, boys?" Chuck's voice boomed through the entire mess hall, too big and ugly for this rustic space. He clocked one of the boys on the shoulder, then led them toward the group of girls.

Chuck and his group of boys stopped in front of their table. Chuck beamed down at Max, like he couldn't believe his good fortune. "What a nice surprise, Maxi Pad," Chuck said. "I didn't expect to see a friendly face."

Max thought she might hurl.

# CHAPTER FOUR

Tanya's eyes were like ice, sharp and cold and unwelcoming. "Camp Neverland is a safe space."

Chuck rolled his long-lashed eyes and ribbed the brunette guy standing next to him. "Safe space, huh, Dave?" His voice took on a whiny, mocking tone. "Last I checked we still have freedom of speech. Not my fault everyone is a sensitive snowflake who can't take a joke." He shrugged.

The tall, slender boy next to him—Dave—looked like he'd rather be anywhere else. His cheeks bloomed bright red, and he ran his fingers through his dark brown hair.

Tanya's presence was impenetrable as cool steel. "There are rules."

"You hear that, Dave? There are *rules*," Chuck mocked. Dave didn't reply, but he looked embarrassed. "You're fun."

Max burst from the table and the food trays rattled. She removed herself awkwardly from the bench and ran toward the bathroom, tears stinging her eyes. She tried to slow her breathing, but the edges of her vision tinged black. A panic attack was imminent. Max barely made it to the bathroom before she began to sob.

A girl with brown skin and dark curls washed her hands in the sink and eyed Max in the mirror. Max slinked into the bathroom's back corner and avoided the girl's eyes. The whole point of camp was to get away from Chuck for a summer. But now he was here, a violation of everything.

Max felt her cellphone in her pocket. Max pulled it out and remembered she had no service. That had been one of the selling points after all.

And what could her mom do, anyway? The camp tuition was non-refundable. Max would be trapped here with Chuck for a whole summer. She put her phone back in her pocket and tried unsuccessfully to get a handle on her erratic breath, to slow her tears.

The bathroom door opened. Great. Her first day at camp and this was her impression.

Max saw through the watery smear through her eyes that it was Tanya. She wiped her snotty nose with her jacket sleeve. "Sorry."

"Why?" Tanya's voice was tender.

"You don't understand," Max said, voice strained, chest heaving. "Everything is ruined."

"You two know each other."

"That's one way of putting it."

"You're here now." Tanya squeezed Max's shoulder firmly. "Camp Neverland is special."

Max scoffed. "They let Chuck in. I thought you said it was like 'so selective' or whatever."

Tanya eyes were beguiling, her slow mannerisms mesmerizing. "We'll take care of you," she said, voice smooth as the surface of an undisturbed lake. "Sisterhood is the whole point. Don't worry about him."

"How can there be sisterhood with boys around?" Max groaned. "I should have never come."

"You really believe that?"

Max wiped tears away from her cheeks with the back of her hand. "I don't know. I had *hoped* it would be wonderful."

"It *is* wonderful," Tanya insisted, eyes glazed over. "We *need* the boys."

"What do you mean, 'need them?'" Max snapped. "Clearly the whole selection process is flawed. This camp can't be that amazing if a guy like Chuck can just waltz in here like he does everywhere else in his life."

Tanya shook her head. "Give us a chance."

"The chance to *what*?"

"Show you."

Max thought again about calling her mom, but she couldn't. Her only real choice was to face Chuck alone, or with allies. She finally nodded. "He's the *worst*," she said.

Tanya squeezed her shoulder again, then let go. "Screw him," she said. "Do you trust me?"

Max met Tanya's eyes, this girl she barely knew, and realized—

"Yeah," she said. "I do."

Tanya's translucent eyes glittered. "Good. Back to the table?"

"I can't." Max's bottom lip quivered. "Not just yet."

Tanya nodded. "Right," she said. "Why don't you head back to the cabin? When we finish, we'll meet you there. I'll sneak some food back, too. We won't want to miss the campfire stories tonight." She grinned. "It's tradition."

# CHAPTER FIVE

Back in Cabin 13, Max drew in her sketchbook. This one was a drawing of Chuck's skinny friend Dave, skin flayed and nailed to the outside of the mess hall building. It was risky, of course, but nothing had ever happened with extreme drawings like this. So far, the only drawings she'd had issues with were on a much smaller scale.

Still, it wasn't the most responsible decision to make the likeness so precise—but the image had appeared so strongly, so forcefully in her head that she had to commit it to paper. Dave had seemed nice enough, but she wasn't sure how anyone truly good could willfully be friends with Chuck.

She sketched until she got chilly.

Max was pulling on an old *X-Files* sweatshirt from the '90s when the three other girls arrived. The sweatshirt belonged to her dad, but Max had swiped it because *X-files* was cool again. Her cabinmates wafted into the space in a bustle of laughter and chatter. Max pulled her red mane from the sweatshirt's neck hole. She hurried to close her sketchbook. Her peers didn't tend to react well to her gruesome drawings.

"Good call on the sweatshirt," Jules said, pushing a strand of purple hair behind her ear. She had the same snake tattoo as Tanya and Izzy, and Max suspected Violet had one as well. She wanted to ask if the tatoos represented some sort of friendship pact, but she didn't. Jules continued: "Vermont summers are warm during the day but cool at night."

"I love it," Max said. "In New Jersey when it's hot, it's just hot. Day and night. That heat will choke you."

"Ooooh, we have ourselves a Jersey girl," Violet said. Her voice could *almost* be described as mousy, except it had an undertone of sharp clarity that dared anyone to call her weak.

Tanya grinned. "I, for one, would love some of that summer heat. I'm always cold."

"Spoken like a true wraith," Izzy said with a flip of her dark braids.

Each of the girls went to their respective bunks to collect sweatshirts and sweaters.

"So, Max," Tanya said, "what was with the whole 'maxi pad' thing?"

Max groaned and lay back on her bunk. She pressed her forearm to her forehead. "It's super embarrassing."

"Try us," Izzy said. "You name it, we've probably been through it, or at least *heard* it."

Max slid her forearm down her face, so it created a shield over her eyes. "I started my period in front of the whole school," she said. "Well, a whole class, anyway. Chuck was there, and he told everyone."

"How awful of him," Violet cooed, then her voice hardened. "Typical ignorant boy."

"Okay, but what's embarrassing about a period?"

Tanya said. "They're just a part of life. Girls have periods."

"That's one benefit of being a girl with a dick," Jules said. "No period for me, thank the goddesses."

"Ugh," Max groaned. "You're lucky." Her insides felt like warm honey. Being surrounded by these empathetic girls was healing on its own. The weight of years of bullying was evaporating from her shoulders.

"You can't let him have power over you," Izzy said.

"I don't *let* him have anything," Max said. "He just takes."

"Most boys do." Tanya shrugged. "But you have us now."

A terrible wave of conflicting emotions surged inside Max. Summer wouldn't last forever. When the summer was over, she'd have to go back to the real world, and Chuck along with her. "I've never—I don't have many friends at home."

The other girls exchanged knowing glances. "Many?" Izzy said.

"Okay, fine," Max said. It was like they'd known each other their whole lives. "Any."

Jules finished tying the laces of her Doc Martens and stood up straight. "That changes now."

"Yeah," Izzy said. "We're yours."

"Friends for *life*," Violet said. "If you'll have us."

*For life.* A chill gripped Max's spine. She burrowed deeply into her sweatshirt for warmth. "You *say* that..."

The girls moved as a group toward the cabin door, Tanya in the lead. She looked back at Max over her shoulder, translucent blue eyes ghostly in the hazy summer twilight. "You're just like us."

The cabin's screen door creaked when she flung it open, and the group stepped out in the summer evening.

—

The trail to the campfire circle was dark, but no one turned on a flashlight. The darkness from the forest closed in. Izzy nudged Max gently in the ribs. "Look up," she whispered.

The tall trees that lined the path formed a dark silhouette against the twilight, but that wasn't the remarkable part. The deep purple-blue sky was already brilliant with stars. The moon appeared larger than usual, milky white and full. Max stopped walking, mouth gaping open.

"It's something else, huh?" Violet's voice was hushed and reverent.

"I've never seen so many," Max murmured.

"Most of us hadn't," Jules said. "Nothing like the Vermont sky at night."

"And the moon," Max said. "It makes me feel so..."

"Magical?" Izzy suggested. "Like anything is possible?"

"Small." The word was an exhale for Max, a sigh of relief. "Like nothing matters."

When Max peeled her eyes away from the glittering stars and met the shining eyes of the four other girls in the twilit dark, she was met with empathy, with understanding. They knew exactly what she met, and for the first time ever, Max felt deeply, wonderfully, exquisitely at home.

"Come on," Tanya said. "The s'mores are calling my name."

The group continued on the path and Max watched fireflies light up around them. They blinked in and out, and Max inhaled the pine scent of the forest and the campfire smell that wafted toward them. It was like a fairy wonderland.

When they reached the clearing by the lake, a huge campfire was already blazing at the center of  large circular rows of wooden folding chairs.

The same men dressed in khaki ranger uniforms Max had seen earlier tended the fire. They took turns adding sticks of firewood to the blaze, faces placid with tight, close-lip smiles. When they weren't tending the fire, they stood in a line at the edge of the woods, their hands clasped in front of them.

Most of the other campers were already gathered, with some happily munching s'mores in their chairs and others standing around the fire, roasting sweet treats. The space buzzed with excited chatter. Bullfrog croaks and cricket song echoed up from the shimmering lake.

A folding table filled with ingredients for s'mores stood along the water's edge. Tanya handed Max a metal stick for her marshmallow, and Max impaled a fat one.

The girls found a clear space around the edge of the huge campfire and hovered the puffy white treats over the flames. The air was filled with the sweet caramel smell of roasting sugar. Max's nostrils filled with the aromas of campfire smoke, burnt sugar, and sharp pine. The campfire popped and crackled.

Then Max tingled with the sensation of being watched, and she scanned the faces of the seated campers. That's when she saw that he was watching her.

Chuck's beautiful, vacant eyes bored into her, a nonconsensual violation. She shivered and hunched into herself.

When they'd finished making s'mores, they found five empty chairs.

A tall, lanky woman wearing a green and white track suit stepped to the fire and faced the campers. Her wiry brown curls were pulled into a puffy ponytail and her wide eyes looked like they might pop out of her head. Her skin was ruddy and tanned and her eyes had a wild look about them. Max's mom may have gone too far in calling her creepy, but Miss Flo definitely had an untamed vibe.

"Hello, campers!" Miss Flo's clear voice carried well in the falling night. She circled the fire slowly, making eye contact with the campers. The murmur of excited chatter slowly faded. "Welcome to another beautiful summer.

"As is tradition here at Camp Neverland, we begin the summer with the annual retelling of a local legend." Miss Flo's eyes widened, a gesture that was supposed to indicate mystery, but which only made her look wackier in the flickering light. "A good, old-fashioned ghost story around the campfire."

Nervous laughter rippled through the captive

audience. A light breeze passed over them, sending a tornado of orange-red embers up into the darkening sky.

Tanya nudged Max's foot with the toe of her sneaker. Max's gaze met those icy blue eyes, and Tanya raised her eyebrows and grinned. "Listen closely," she whispered. "This is the best part."

"Once on these lands, there lived a man and a woman," Miss Flo began. "They married, as was customary, but they weren't in love, as was common. Upon marriage, they moved into an unassuming log cabin—right here in these woods."

Tanya's breath was hot against Max's ear. "It's still there," she whispered. "It's where Miss Flo stays."

Max looked at Tanya, full of questions. But Miss Flo was still talking. Max's curiosity would have to wait.

"It began quietly," Miss Flo said. "First, she stood up to him in the privacy of their home. She challenged his power. He didn't like it, but he hoped for offspring to continue the family line, so he tolerated her defiance. At first."

Miss Flo paused here for effect. The firelight flickered. Light and shadow slithered across her face. Max shivered and pulled her sweatshirt tighter.

"Then she became more public with her disdain," Miss Flo continued. "She began challenging him in front of others, arguing with his logic, mocking him openly. He felt humiliated, to be so publicly degraded by a woman, his wife no less, the woman who was supposed to submit to him."

Max looked at the faces of her cabinmates, flickering in the orange glow cast by the fire. They watched Miss Flo with unfiltered adoration, rapt expressions on their faces, eyes shining. But Miss Flo was still speaking, so Max turned her attention back to the story.

"One night, after a particularly humiliating evening in the village, during which the man had also had his fill of drink, the couple had a horrific fight when they returned home to their cabin. She was strong and sturdy in her own right, but ultimately, he overpowered her—in both strength and size. I'm sorry to say, he beat her. She kept eye contact with him the whole time, blood leaking from her mouth, down her chin. She grinned, her teeth stained red, and taunted him. 'Go ahead and kill me,' she said.

"Her taunt was the last straw. He wanted to humiliate her the way she had humiliated him. The man was drunk and full of rage. He didn't pause to consider the consequences of his actions, as men rarely do. He grabbed his axe from beside the front door and in one fell swoop, he chopped her head clean off. Her head hit the wooden floor with a heavy thud and rolled to face him, her eyes wide open, watching, mocking him—perhaps, even, still seeing him—in death.

"He was instantly filled with remorse—not for killing her, but for fear of being discovered and punished for his actions by the townspeople. So, he dug a hole deep within these woods. He threw her lifeless body and head into the hole—along with the bloodied axe—and filled it with dirt."

Miss Flo paused. Max tensed with dread.

"In the night," Miss Flo continued, "the woman's spirit cried out to the land, anguished and enraged. The snakes of the forest heard her pleas and came to her—hundreds of them. They found her body, buried in the earth, and they burrowed down through the soil. The snakes filled her, knitting her body back together with theirs. They writhed inside of her and reanimated her, helped her dig her way up and out of her grave. The woman and the snakes moved as one. Together, they reached for the axe and found their way back to the cabin, where the man slept with a peace only afforded by the unrepentant. The snakes and the woman raised the axe over their head with both arms. They brought the gleaming axe head down upon the unsuspecting man—a silver mouth hungry for revenge. When they were done, they scattered the chunks of his body outside the cabin for the forest creatures to feast upon."

Miss Flo paused, circling the campfire, wild eyes searching the campers stunned faces. "It is said," Miss Flo continued, "that she still wanders these woods, a woman-like creature filled with snakes, insatiably hungry for the blood of men."

# CHAPTER SIX

Miss Flo's story did what all good ghost stories should: it cast a spell of dread over the campers. An eerie vibe descended in the middle of the Vermont forest.

One by one, the campers left the wooden chairs behind and trickled onto the dirt paths that cut through the woods, hushed voices carrying in the night. The Cabin 13 bunk mates huddled close together on the path in the dark.

"Tell me again why we don't have a flashlight?" Max whispered.

"Blame Tanya," Izzy said. "She likes to be 'one with the night.'"

Tanya scoffed and poked Izzy's side. "Like I'm the only one," she said. "Miss Astrology."

"It's fun to find the constellations," Izzy retorted.

"True," Jules said. "Your eyes adjust to the dark better without a flashlight. And anyway, I get most of my inspiration at night."

Max glanced up again at the spatter of stars above the trail. "I never knew stars could be so bright."

"They get even brighter," Violet said. "Especially in the middle of the night."

"So, what's up with that story?" Max said. "It can't be *true*, right?"

Violet, resident mythology nerd, giggled in the dark. "The best stories make you wonder," she said. "That's why folklore is so powerful."

"The cabin..." Max said.

"The cabin is real," Jules said.

"Okay," Max said. "But it can't be the *same* cabin?"

"Why not?" Tanya said.

Max pulled her sweatshirt tighter, suddenly realizing how cold she was. "All right, but the bit about the snakes..."

"That's the magic of legends," Violet said.

Izzy groaned. "Don't get her started."

"What?" Violet said, playfully defensive.

"Oh, come on." Tanya said. They teased each other, but it was all affectionate. Max basked in the warmth that emanated off their love for one another.

"But seriously," Jules said, "if you thought that was good, just wait 'til Initiation."

"What's that?" Max said.

"A secret," Tanya said, prodding Jules playfully.

"Oh, stop that," Violet laughed. "It's on the New Moon, when first-time campers are initiated."

"That sounds..." Max wanted to say *creepy*, but instead she said, "...mysterious."

"Camp wouldn't be as fun if there weren't a few surprises," Izzy said.

They arrived at Cabin 13 and pushed the screen door open. Tanya reached for the pull string and clicked on the main overhead light. Several white, ethereal moths fluttered around at the disturbance before settling on the door's screen.

Violet shrugged. "Stories make us," she said. "Without them, we're no different than other animals."

The girls headed to their individual bunks, each

searching through their things for pajamas. Max traded her worn jeans for her favorite baggy sweatpants.

Jules tossed her cardigan onto the bed. "*That* I do agree with." She pulled a small black velvet bag tied with a drawstring from the wicker nightstand next to her bunk. "Which is why I *love* tarot."

Max raised an eyebrow and Tanya grinned. "Ever had a reading?" she said.

"No."

Violet beamed from where she had already settled onto her bunk, knees tucked up against her chin. "Jules is really good."

"The best," Izzy said.

"There was a psychic at the mall once a couple year ago," Max said. "But my mom wouldn't give me money. Said it was satanic."

Jules snorted. "Please. That's such old paradigm bullshit. No offense to your mom. It's not her fault society perpetuates such fear-based superstitions," she said. "With a mall psychic, odds are the worst you have to worry about is she's a scam."

Izzy pulled on an old Pink Floyd sweatshirt, smeared with old pottery stains and lay back onto her bunk's mattress. "And now you've gone and got *her* started," she said, and laughed. "We're about to be up all night. Also, who goes to malls still?"

Jules climbed onto her bunk and sat cross-legged on the mattress. She slipped her tarot deck from the velvet pouch and began to shuffle the cards. She eyed Max squarely. "Want a card?" she said.

Max shrugged, nervous but intrigued. "Yeah, okay," she said.

Jules shuffled the deck a few more times, the cards swishing and fluttering rhythmically between her palms. Then, without any cue that Max could see, she stopped and flipped the top card over.

Max, unfamiliar with tarot, stared at the card. The card's illustration featured a person carrying a long tilted cane or stick, with six other sticks in the ground blocking their way forward. "What's it mean?" she said.

"Seven of wands," Jules said, and the three other girls observed from their bunks. "It's you against the world."

Max prickled, suddenly too vulnerable. "Maybe sometimes it is."

Jules shrugged. "Here's the thing," she said. "Most people interpret this card as meaning there is actual, true opposition. People out to get you, you've got to defend yourself. All that."

"Sounds about right," Max mumbled.

"It sounds right because most of us feel like that in some form or another," Jules said. "But what if there's more to it?"

"How so?"

"What if it's about our internal lives?" Jules caressed the card with a slender finger. "We put so much effort into protecting ourselves, guarding our hearts, afraid to let anyone in."

"No one ever wanted in before," Max whispered. "Unless it was to hurt me."

"Key word there: *before*," Jules nodded. "This card is here *now*. Your defenses are still up, but it's time to look around."

Max looked around at her four cabinmates, each curled up on their minimalist mattresses, watching her, faces beaming.

"You're here now. With us," Jules continued. "We see you, and we want to know you. It's safe to let your guard down."

Jules held eye contact with Max, who barely resisted the urge to run from this cabin and never look back. It wasn't because Jules wasn't right—it's because she was, and the vulnerability was almost unbearable. She was used to being invisible and being seen was a new and overwhelming sensation.

The shrill cricket song amplified a chorus through the screens. A moth in the doorway fluttered briefly by the light. Max searched the faces of her cabinmates. They gave her space to process Jules' reading, didn't rush her into talking or sharing. Tears burned the corners of Max's eyes and she struggled to hold them in, still afraid after everything.

Everyone in the cabin was quiet for another long moment, the nocturnal sounds of the forest filling up the small space with night.

Then, finally, Izzy grinned. "See?" she said. "Told you she was good."

Her comment dissolved the pressure Max felt to respond, and the five girls burst into laughter. Still warm from laughing, Max slipped into her sleeping bag on top of her mattress and curled her arm beneath her pillow. It felt as though her heart was expanding in her chest. She had hoped camp would be a reprieve, but she had never dared to hope it would be *this* good.

The sweet, piercing sound of a bell echoed through the forest.

"Light's out," Tanya explained. She got out of her bunk and reached for the pull string on their main overhead light. The room melted into darkness. "I recommend a good night's sleep."

"She's right," Violet said. "It's hard to sleep the first night, but we'll need it."

"Truth," Izzy said.

Then Jules voice rose up in the dark: "Max, ready for the first day of the rest of your life?"

Max grinned in the dark and settled against her pillow. Her thoughts were an endless whir, anticipating what the morning might bring.

But none of her racing thoughts truly prepared her for what awaited them at dawn. Because, when they arrived at the mess hall for breakfast, they discovered the first body.

# CHAPTER SEVEN

It was Dave, the tall, brunette boy who'd come to their table last night with Chuck. He was naked, body nailed to the front of the mess hall in the shape of a cross, the flesh on his palms and tops of his feet punctured with nails that dug right into the rustic wooden logs of the building's exterior. His blood was drying and blackened in the mounting heat of the morning sunlight, flesh already rancid with rot. His head hung down over his chest. Flies buzzed greedily over his wounds.

Max cried out and clutched her notebook. Fear clawed at her insides.

The scene was identical to one she had drawn last night. She should have been more careful. Things had never gone this far before—but it had still been a careless choice.

The stink from the body was obscene. She covered her mouth and nose with her hand.

The other girls encircled Max, bodies pressed against hers, a human shield. They spoke in hushed, soothing whispers, telling her she was alright, it would be okay.

Max was nauseous. It was surprisingly warm for this early in the morning; the sun beat down so fiercely on the top of her head it burned. She realized she'd forgotten to put on sunscreen.

Bile rose at the back of Max's throat. This was *her* fault.

The other girls shushed and soothed her, hands roving softly over her arms, smoothing her hair.

"Let's get inside," Tanya said.

"But—he's—" Max couldn't bring herself to say it.

Jules voice was close against her ear. "I know. It'll be

okay."

Max let them herd into the mess hall. They helped her sit on a bench at one of the sprawling cafeteria tables. She felt as though she was outside her body. Izzy brought her a red plastic cup filled with cold water, and she gulped it down.

Once they were all seated, Max looked at their faces, dazed, uncertain. They were smiling. *Smiling.*

Max blinked several times, trying to clear her head. The girls could never know about the drawing. They would fear her, just like the kids at school did. This had been a chance for a fresh start, and Max had ruined it. She swallowed the rest of the water.

"We should—we should—" Max shoved her hand into her pocket to retrieve her phone. She fumbled with it for a moment before she remembered that she didn't have any cell service here in these green Vermont mountains. Briefly, she thought back to the camp brochure. 'No cell service' was listed as a perk—an opportunity to become truly immersed in nature and art, to disconnect from the constant pull of technology, the incessant toxicity of social media. With a twist in her gut, Max remembered the allure of this, the relief of the imagined break. And now—

"I don't have service." A statement of fact.

Jules leaned into her on the bench. "Max, put it away."

The mess hall filled with other campers, their clamoring voices buzzing with alarm.

"Shouldn't we—do something?" Max whispered.

Tanya's blond brows furrowed. "Let's start with you," she said. "Take deep breaths."

Max tried, but the traces of the boy's death stink still filled her nostrils. She felt the urge to be sick again. She squeezed her eyes shut, but all she saw was the drawing in her sketchbook. The knowledge of its presence in her backpack burned into her conscience. "This was a mistake."

"What was?" Violet said, brown eyes liquid concern behind her glasses.

"Coming here," Max said. She couldn't tell them about the drawing. "How are you all so...calm?" Max slipped closer to the edge of pure panic.

"We're not new." Izzy sipped her water. "Miss Flo takes care of everything. You'll see."

"A boy is *dead*." Max's voice elevated to a shriek.

"It's scary, I know," Jules said. "But you don't have to carry it. Be a kid, you know? The adults'll handle it."

"But doesn't it at least—" Max paused. "Freak you out?"

"He probably deserved it," Violet said, shockingly passive. "After all, he's friends with that guy you hate."

"No one deserves...that," Max said, voice edged with shame. "And I don't *hate* him."

"You don't have to be a proper young lady with us," Tanya said, eyebrow raised. "You can say what you mean."

"It's not that I hate him." Max bit her lip. "I just want him to leave me alone. It's the only thing I've *ever* wanted. Not..."

"Hey, the line is filling up," Izzy said. "Let's eat."

Max looked from her cabinmates to the lines forming along the cafeteria stations and blinked several times. The girls seemed unphased and unbothered, despite the dead human body crucified to the outside of that very building.

"I know it's strange," Tanya said, voice soothing as cool water. "It's like Izzy said. We've been here...a long time. Miss Flo takes care of us. You can relax. Rest. Like Jules' reading last night, you know? You don't need to be hypervigilant. You're safe."

Warmth spread through Max, the sick feeling in her belly slowly replaced with a warm honey sensation. She looked down at the phone in her hand. The girls were right. The drawing was probably just a terrible coincidence, anyway. Just like all the others. Hadn't Jules said it? *Be a kid.* Let the adults clean up the mess, for once. She sighed deeply.

"Look," Violet said.

Miss Flo had just stepped through the mess hall's great double doors, curly hair pulled back into a tight bun, wearing a purple track suit this morning. She walked with purpose toward the front of the hall.

"Good morning, campers," Miss Flo said, voice somber but commanding. "You've all seen the unfortunate—*situation* outside."

"That's one way of putting it," Max muttered.

"There is no reason for worry or concern." Her voice was sweet and liquid, seducing and certain. "We've called the proper channels and an investigation is imminent. In the meantime, please, don't let this dampen your spirits. Here at Camp Neverland, we provide you with reprieve and escape. Nothing has changed."

The sound of Miss Flo's voice soothed and lulled Max. Her head felt dreamy, and her stomach had that warm-honey-feel again.

But something was still bothering Max, still nagging at her, like a thorn caught beneath her skin. It pressed gently against the inside of her chest.

Miss Flo's voice drifted toward them like a dream. "So, please," she was saying, "enjoy yourselves. Relax. Eat your breakfast. It's the first official day of camp, and that should be celebrated. You'll need fuel for the day's activities. Leave this to us. My men are outside now, cleaning up. It's unfortunate, but don't let this ruin your day."

Then, miraculously, Miss Flo's gaze settled right onto Max. Her eyes reminded Max of a lizard. "We are here for *you*. And we are here to keep you safe. Can you trust us to do that?"

When Miss Flo stopped speaking, there was momentary silence in the mess hall, with no other sounds than those of the kitchen staff cooking and preparing food. Then the room erupted into applause, escalating with whoops and hollers. Max joined in on the clapping.

"Good," Miss Flo said, beaming. "You won't regret it. Now, come, let's forget this nonsense and get on with our day!"

She left the front of the room and the noise of conversation and the shuffle of sneakers on the concrete floor began as more campers headed up to the cafeteria line.

Max and her group headed up together, and Max felt like she was glowing. She felt high.

The girls stood in line with their trays, waiting to get their food.

"Today should be warm enough for a swim," Tanya said.

"I'm still sunburned from last week," Violet said.

"I've got extra sunscreen," Izzy said.

"Who do you think killed him?" Max said, interrupting.

She may have drawn the picture, but someone still had to nail the boy to the front of the building.

Violet shrugged and placed a fat piece of chicken sausage onto her plate using tongs. "Who knows. They'll handle it."

Max eyed the food and her stomach turned on her. All she could think about was the boy's flesh cooking outside in the warm morning sun. "But who's *they*?"

"You heard Miss Flo," Tanya said. "She's got this."

Max fell silent. She scanned their faces, bewildered by their visages of absolute calm. "But—" Max started, and Izzy shot her a look. "Shouldn't they leave his body up until the authorities have had a chance to investigate?"

"They took pictures," Jules said. "Do you think it's better to leave him up? Look how it's affecting you.

Imagine if he was just up there all day, rotting?" She shuddered.

"It'll be okay," Izzy said, voice soothing, "Really."

The girls carried their trays back to their table and sat down.

"You know how many dead girls turn up in the world and people barely notice?" Jules said with a shrug. "It's probably just the scales tipping a bit."

"Aren't you worried at all?" Max said.

"About?" Tanya said.

"There's someone killing kids and nailing them to buildings," Max said. "Who's to say next time it won't be a girl? Or one of us?"

"Who's to say there will be a next time?" Violet said.

Max felt like she was missing something crucial, some missing piece of the puzzle that would help her relax if only she could find it. She eyed the food on her plate. The room started to spin and she put her head in her hands.

Max felt a hand on her back. "I'm sorry." Tanya's voice was gentle again. "It's easy for us to forget."

"Forget what?" Max said.

"It's your first time."

# CHAPTER EIGHT

The honeyed sunlight graced the campground's expanse of green grass and forest. The aromas of tangy pine and sweet honeysuckle and warm grass were thick in the air, dizzying and electrifying. The events of the morning felt far away, if not unimportant.

Max was intoxicated by the clear sweet mountain air, charmed by the buzz of fat bumblebees and the lazy drifting of puffy white clouds across the sharp blue sky. Camp Neverland was enchanting and Max allowed it to bewitch and seduce her.

She had spent the rest of the morning in the center for visual artists, surrounded by other skilled creators. She was bent over her sketchbook, furiously working on her comic. The center also provided new mediums for her to experiment with, high quality paints and markers and pens she'd never tried before.

Back home, it was Chuck who'd figured out what was happening.

In one of her comic series, Max had made herself a teen witch. She was the hero, her thinly veiled classmates the unapologetic villains. She had always drawn the bad things she *wished* would happen to them, so that was nothing new. But after the period incident, everything had changed.

And once Max knew what she was capable of, she started experimenting.

It had been harmless things, at first.

Bright bulbous pimples on their noses at prom. Lost

football games with embarrassingly low scores. Toilet paper on the bottoms of their shoes.

But then Kristi Peterson—the head cheerleader—had put the dead bird she'd found in the courtyard in Max's unruly red curls. She'd done it in the middle of English class, and Max had been working on a sketch so intensely she hadn't noticed. Not until lunchtime, and by then, it was far too late.

Furious, and without any way of having any real revenge, Max took out her anger on a drawing of Kristi Peterson falling from the top of a cheerleading pyramid and breaking her leg.

A few days later Chuck caught her in the hallway, Kristi ambling in a leg cast next to him, and pried the sketchbook from her hands. Chuck had flipped through the pages carelessly, exposing her drawings to a hall full of snickering teenagers. It had all been the usual torment 'til he discovered the drawing of Kristi—and saw that the date scrawled at the bottom of the page was before the accident.

Psycho. Witch. Freak.

Max had been more careful after that.

Here at camp, Max knew she couldn't take any more chances.

This afternoon, she was revisiting the drawing of the dead boy, the sweet sunlight splashing in across her artist's desk. She embellished the details. He was already dead, after all.

Tanya was in a corner at her easel with the other painters, where she painted colorful and elaborate sigils.

Jules, a skilled collage artist designing her own tarot deck, sat at the desk next to Max's.

There was a commotion at the entrance.

Max looked up. It was Chuck.

She was about to duck her head down, but something about Chuck's face made her keep looking. He wasn't wearing his usual cold mask of indifference. His eyes were wild, like a trapped horse. His cheeks were flushed pink and his usually smooth-coifed hair was a tousled mess.

Max's breath caught in her chest and twisted like a knife. The worst thing about Chuck was his beauty. His eyes glittered; his hair fell in his eyes just right. He was the star of everything—captain of the football team, but smart too, with perfect grades. Students loved him, teachers loved him, everyone loved him. He got away with everything by flashing that beautiful smile in just the right way. It was all annoyingly cliché.

All that beauty, all that charm, wasted. It would be better if he'd been hideous—an exterior to match his interior. But that would have been too easy.

He had never looked so human as he did then, the truth written all over his face. A warm liquid rush of compassion flooded through Max, heart betraying her. She would forgive him in an instant. She didn't *want* an enemy.

Chuck's eyes snagged on hers. Max thought maybe that was the first time he was really *seeing* her. She swallowed. And then Chuck's expression curdled. The spell was broken.

Chuck was heading over to her desk, looking meaner than ever. She'd caught him in a vulnerable moment, and he was going to punish her.

Max slammed her sketchbook shut on top of her pencil.

Chuck stopped in front of her, arms crossed over his puffed-out chest, looking down his chiseled nose at her and her closed book. "What're you hiding, Maxi-Pad?"

Max tried to remember what Tanya had said before about periods not being embarrassing. It was only an insult if she let it be one. "Sorry about your friend."

"Barely knew him," Chuck shrugged. "Better him than me, right?"

"Better no one," Max said.

"Sure," Chuck said. "As long I'm not the one dead."

Max glanced over at Jules, who had paused work on her collage to watch the interaction. "Why are you even here?"

Chuck's upper lip curled. "I have as much right to come to summer camp as anyone else."

"But why *this* camp?" Max said. "I didn't even know you liked art."

"There's a lot you don't know about me." Chuck's voice was bare, honest. Mean as he was, he really meant that.

"I picture you at like football camp or something."

"Awwww, Maxi-Pad." Chuck ran his fingers through his tousled hair and winked. "You picture me?"

Max stared at her desk, cheeks burning. "I didn't mean...that's not what I..."

She squirmed. She should be immune to his looks, knowing what she knew about his heart.

"Listen," Chuck said, "I got this fucking pamphlet, right? And it sounded...too good to be true. I had to check it out."

Max's insides soured with the bitter tang of betrayal. When she had received the pamphlet in the mail, it had felt like magic. The only thing better would have been a flying boy in green landing on her windowsill, whisking her away to a magical land. Now she saw she'd been a total fool.

"What's this?" Chuck grabbed Max's sketchbook and yanked it off her desk. She reached for the pages, but she didn't want to rip them.

"Give it back," Max muttered.

"You sick fuck." Chuck had the notebook splayed opened to where her pencil had kept her spot, displaying its contents in a way that made Max feel more vulnerable than if she'd been naked.

If her cabinmates saw the picture, it wasn't a big deal.

But Chuck knew her secrets. He would expose her.

"What the *fuck*?" Chuck's face was red, nostrils flaring. He dangled the notebook in Max's face, so close her nose almost touched the page. "You did this?

"Hey." This from Jules, on her way to Max's desk. "What's the problem?"

Chuck flipped the notebook around, so the open spread faced Jules. "You see this shit?"

Jules flicked her eyes, glittering like sapphire

stones, to the page and shrugged. "First of all, this is art camp," she said. "Second of all, most art is inspired by real life. It's not remarkable."

Max bristled. Her sketches were personal, living, breathing journal entries. It was weird hearing people talk about her drawings so casually.

As though on cue, Jules turned to Max and said, "The subject matter isn't remarkable, but your skills are."

Chuck turned the notebook back around and eyed the pages. "You don't know your friend like I do," he said to Jules. "She's into some satanic occult shit. But I didn't know she'd go this far."

Max's heart raced.

Jules fluttered her eyelids, a mock-flirtatious expression. "You had me at satanic."

Max suddenly realized how absurd Chuck's accusations sounded. A smile crept over her face.

"It's art." Max made a grab for the sketchbook and Chuck pulled it back, just out of her reach. "Not like you'd understand."

"You don't know shit about me." Chuck turned his eyes back to her drawing. "Lemme take a wild guess— you drew this picture *before* he was dead, right?"

His eyes glued to the paper again and Max saw her chance. She snatched the sketchbook from his hands. One of the pages ripped.

"I don't know what you're talking about." Max had erased the date from the bottom of the drawing.

"She doesn't need to defend her art to anyone,"

Jules said, arms crossed over her chest. "Especially not you, *bro.*"

"Who asked you?" Chuck said. "You're both freaks."

"Grow up," Max snapped.

"Well, well, well, look who grew some balls. These people don't know yet what a psycho witch freak you are. They'll piss you off soon enough and end up in one of your sick drawings..."

"We don't tolerate hate speech at Camp Neverland, young man."

Chuck whirled around. Miss Flo towered over him. He held up his hands.

"Hey, now, hey," Chuck said. "No hate speech here. Just speaking facts."

Miss Flo raised an eyebrow and looked at Max and Jules. "Girls?"

"He's a dick," Jules said, sapphire eyes sharp enough to cut.

Max nodded. "He took my sketchbook."

"If you're worried about anyone, it should be her," Chuck said. "She's the—the witch. She drew the dead kid. She draws bad things happening to people she hates, and then they happen."

Max tried not to smile. Chuck was the one who sounded like a 'psycho freak.'

Miss Flo's mouth was a thin, tight line. "Young man, what you are suggesting is ludicrous. And many of our campers are actual witches," she said. "We don't use that word as a pejorative. We don't judge each other's expression. In art. In spiritual practice. Or otherwise."

"I wasn't judging," Chuck said. "I was—"

"I've had just about enough of your mouth for one afternoon," Miss Flo said. "You signed the papers. You agreed to our Code of Ethics. Did you not read the fine print?"

"Fine...what?" Chuck said.

Miss Flo nodded almost imperceptibly to the two men in khaki ranger uniforms who had just entered the compound. "Well, that's a shame," she said. "You certainly should have."

The two men took Chuck by the arms.

"The fuck?" Chuck shrieked. He yanked his arms to no avail.

Miss Flo nodded again. "Some time alone to think will help you reevaluate your behavior," she said. "For your sake, I hope you do."

The men began to escort Chuck from the building. "She's the one you want," he shouted. "That psycho witch *freak*. You'll see."

"Please, young man." Miss Flo examined a neatly manicured nail, bored. "Don't make a scene."

"I'll call my mom!" Chuck shouted as the men dragged him out the door. "I'll call my lawyer!"

Miss Flo smiled coyly. "With what phone?" she said. "For that matter, you and your parents signed the same contract. You all agreed to these terms."

"What *terms*?" Chuck's voice echoed through the front door, but he was gone.

Miss Flo turned back to Max and Jules. "I apologize you had to witness that...unpleasantness," she said.

"Camp Neverland is a safe space for *all*—but particularly for young women."

Max swallowed. "Where are you taking him?"

"Don't you waste one minute worrying about him," Miss Flo said sweetly. "I suspect you've done enough of that already."

Despite all Chuck had done to torment her, Max didn't want him *harmed*. "But—"

"Many boys aren't taught the importance of 'safe spaces,'" Miss Flo continued. "That's because they're often the threat. Some boys just need a little extra...teaching. That's all."

A shiver went through Max. "What are they going to...?"

"My girl, please don't worry." Miss Flo's eyes glittered. "They will simply... *teach* him."

"But how—?"

Miss Flo clucked her tongue. "Enough." The word was firm, but her voice kind. She glanced at Max's open sketchbook and the corners of her mouth turned up slightly. "You have a drawing to finish."

# CHAPTER NINE

The girls sat at a table in the mess hall for lunch. Tanya looked annoyed for the first time since Max had met her, and the other three girls poked at their food.

"Why do you even care what happens to him?" Tanya said.

Max shrugged. "He's mean. But he's a person, too."

Tanya rolled her eyes. "Yeah, and so was Hitler. People need consequences."

"But what did she mean by 'fine print?'" Max said.

Izzy took a tentative bite. "That's between him and the camp."

"It sounded so ominous."

"He violated your space," Tanya said, "Degraded you. Don't you think it's time boys stop getting away with that?"

"Of course I do."

"Stop blaming yourself," Tanya said. "It's what he wants. You've done nothing wrong. He's being held accountable for his own actions."

Max wanted to tell them this was her fault. All of this could have been avoided if she'd just had some self-control. But here in Vermont, in these woods...things just felt right. *Max* felt right. She hadn't thought any of this could happen. She pinched the bridge of her nose between her fingers and squeezed her eyes shut, hoping to stop the tears that threatened to spill.

Tanya's face softened, and the other girls exchanged glances. "I keep forgetting that you're new," Tanya said. "It just feels like you've been with us forever. Trust takes time."

Max bit her quivering bottom lip. "I'm not defending Chuck."

Jules reached across the table, squeezed her hand.

"You know, psychologically, there's a real tendency for people to try to protect their abusers."

Max flinched. She hadn't specifically thought of Chuck in those terms, but hearing Jules say it, she felt a flood of relief. *Abuse.* That's what Chuck had done to her for years.

Tears finally broke free and slid down Max's cheeks. She gritted her teeth.

He *deserved* a wakeup call.

"We just care," Violet said. "We don't want to see you waste your time here worrying about some jerk."

"It's a waste of energy," Izzy added.

Max smeared the tears off her cheeks. She reached for a napkin to blow her nose into. "You're right," she said. "All of you."

"We don't want to be *right.*" Jules squeezed her hand more tightly, arm still extended from across the table. "We've all...known boys like him."

"Yeah?" Max said.

"The world is full of them." Jules lifted her chin. "Boys who make their own rules and expect the rest of us to fall in line."

Max nodded. "I'm tired of being invisible."

"We're *lucky* if we're invisible." Jules spoke softly. "Boys can be very cruel."

Tanya leaned her warm body against Max. "No more wasting energy on that dipshit?"

"No more," Max said.

"Consequences for bad behavior are what keeps Camp Neverland so safe for us," Tanya said. "So welcoming."

*Welcoming.* Max couldn't remember the last time she'd felt welcomed...*anywhere.* Her parents loved her, but her mom was always busy with work. When she was home, she was tired and lost in her own head. Her dad tried, but he was mostly swept up in his new marriage and his new kids.

Max searched the faces of the girls around the table. Perhaps, one day, she could even tell them the truth about the notebooks.

"I trust you," Max said.

And she meant it.

But just as she said it, she remembered a peculiar thing: the authorities had never come to camp that day.

Her cabinmates had resumed laughing, talking, eating. Jules caught Max's eye and offered an encouraging wink. Max smiled back and took a bite of mashed potatoes, then swallowed.

"Ever practiced witchcraft?" Jules said.

"Not...exactly." Max's cheeks burned. "I sometimes light candles, make wishes. I love the *Black Magic* comic. Why?"

"You know," Jules said, "Chuck used 'witch' as a slur. I'd take it as a compliment."

"What he said..." Max couldn't bring herself to finish.

"About your drawings?" Jules said. "Who cares? Besides, art and magic are interconnected."

"They are?" Max said.

"Absolutely," Jules said.

"So then..."

"I use my art to channel magic all the time," Jules said. The other girls around the table nodded.

"You need to cut energetic cords between you and Chuck," Jules said.

"He does have a pull on me," Max said.

"You feel it, right?" Jules said.

Max nodded.

"I thought so," Jules said.

"But how?"

"Lots of ways," Jules said. "A meditation. Or in the shower, let the water wash away the negative bonds. You could literally use your hand and imagine it's a sword slicing through a cord."

"That doesn't sound too hard," Max said.

"It doesn't." Jules tilted her head and brushed a strand of purple hair from her eyes. "You need something stronger, something personal. These cords are strong. The more personal your magic, the more powerful the ritual."

"She knows her shit," Izzy interjected, fingers threaded through her beaded necklace to lift it. "My grandmother gave me this ancestral heirloom. I lost it once—and Jules helped me find it. Way off the trail in the woods!"

"Whoa," Max said.

"To start, you should draw him," Jules said.

"Do I have to draw him like...dead or something?" Max said.

Jules made a face. "What? No," Jules said. "Put as much detail as you can into the drawing. Everything he's ever made you feel. Everything he's ever said or done."

Max shuddered. The thought of drawing Chuck honestly was repulsive.

"That face you just made?" Jules said. "It's how I know we're on the right track."

Max grimaced. "That sounds..."

"Terrible," Jules said, "That's the point, it's what will make the spell effective. Because when you're done? You're going to burn it."

Max's stomach fluttered. She was used to being angry at Chuck and the other kids at school. She was used to giving them worts and pimples and rashes in her drawings—there were other ways she tortured them, but skin issues were just about the worst punishment for a popular, beautiful, superficial teen. But Max had never simply *drawn* any of them.

It did sound cathartic. A regular drawing couldn't hurt Chuck the way another kind of drawing might. "And that will cut the cord?"

"Well, you've got to infuse the spell with your intention," Jules said. "It's as symbolic as it is real. But it will help you release your attachment."

"I'm not attached."

"After that long of being tormented by someone, there are all kinds of attachments between you," Jules said. "Things you're hanging onto, resentments and rage. This will help you let go. Claim who you *are*, without him."

"I'll do it," Max said, determined. "If anything, it will feel good just to..."

"Watch his face burn?" Jules guessed. "Say it. There are plenty of boys I'd gladly watch burn. Remember, you're among friends. We get it."

The girls at the table shared a hearty laugh, and the flutter in Max's stomach burst into a flame. She nurtured that flame all throughout lunch, tending and stoking its sparks until a fire roared.

After lunch, she went to the visual arts compound to draw Chuck. A true, honest drawing. No punishments. She drew with fervor and fury, pouring every last bit of her emotion into the details. Max didn't stop until the drawing was complete.

She held it up into the sunlight and beamed.

It was the best thing she'd ever drawn.

Max tucked the drawing safely into the pages of her sketchbook.

# CHAPTER TEN

Tonight was the night.

Max had wanted to burn the drawing the day she made it, but Jules had insisted she wait until the waning quarter moon because the spell would be more powerful.

The days blurred together in a dreamy haze of warm summer sunlight, the sunbaked aroma of fresh pine, the eerie hum of katydids. Max spent most of her time in the visual arts compound, sketching illustrations.

Their days were largely unstructured, to simulate an artist's lifestyle. Campers were trusted to spend time on their projects as necessary, but they were encouraged to take regular mental breaks. Forest trail walks and dips into the crystal-cool lake were recognized as just as important to the creative process as the time spent in active artistic creation.

Each day ended with a roaring campfire down by the lake. These gatherings were much less structured than the first night. The campers mingled freely. S'mores and hot cocoa were an evening staple.

Max sat in wooden folding chairs by the fire with her group. Violet and Jules munched on s'mores, but the rest had already finished theirs.

Max scanned the campers. Not for the first time, she noticed the figure eight snake tattoo on the insides of the wrists of returning campers, just like her cabinmates. Only the first-time campers, like herself, were without it. Max tingled with a not-unpleasant hum of anticipation.

She suspected the tattoo had something to do with the Initiation. The upcoming event was still shrouded in mystery. Max wasn't sure if it was legal to tattoo teenagers, but she figured there was something in the piles of paperwork her parents had signed, releasing them from being able to take any legal action. The thought of receiving her very first tattoo was thrilling.

Max hadn't seen Chuck since the day the ranger men had dragged him off. The sweets soured in her stomach.

Tonight's cord cutting ceremony couldn't come a moment too soon.

"Earth to Max." Izzy's hair was pulled into a thick dark braid that wrapped over her shoulder. She looked at Max, eyes shining intensely.

"What?" Max said.

"I *said*, you never told me your sign," Izzy said. "We were just talking about our mugs."

The mugs in question were Izzy's specialty, and each girl had one—except for Max. They sipped hot cocoa out of them now. The mugs were astonishing works of ceramic art, with brilliant fire-blazed colors—the deep blues, rich purples, and subdued pinks of the night sky. The astrology constellations carved into the sides were embossed in shimmering gold. They were perfectly glazed and smoothed—a highly coveted commodity among the campers. Izzy charged top dollar for her creations but had gifted one to each girl in their cabin.

"I'm a Leo," Max said.

Izzy nodded. "I totally see it. You've even got that red lion's mane."

"You don't have to make me one."

"What're you talking about, 'have to?'" Izzy snorted. "I don't do anything I don't want to."

"It's true," Tanya said, sipping from her steaming mug. "They're Izzy's pride and joy."

"The constellations are my favorite," Izzy said, beaming. "The gold embossing is an intricate process. When I get it just right? No feeling like it."

"Cool." Max smiled. She reached for her backpack to

retrieve the drawing of Chuck and her stomach sank. In all her excitement for the evening, she'd forgotten to grab her pack on her way out of Cabin 13.

"I'll be right back," she muttered to Izzy.

Izzy lifted an eyebrow. "Feeling left out?"

"I forgot my backpack," Max said.

"It'll be safe in the cabin." Tanya poked Jules in her ribs. "Jules has magical protections all around it."

"It's true," Jules said. "I never go anywhere without my bag of sea salt."

"It's not that," Max said. "It's the drawing."

"Oh, yeah," Jules said. "We need that thing out of the cabin. It's giving me weird vibes."

"Me, too," Max said.

"Want company?" Violet offered.

"No, thanks," Max said. "It'll be faster if I run on my own."

"You sure?" Violet said. "It's dark on the trail."

"I'll be okay," Max said.

"We'll save your seat," Tanya said.

Max nodded and stepped onto the dirt path that led to the larger trail that would take her back to the cabin. Max paused at the trailhead.

A wooden sign that said TO CABINS was skewered into the dirt at the entrance. It was bordered by thick trees on either side, and the darkness was so complete she *almost* doubled back to take Violet up on her offer, after all.

Max glanced up at the twilit sky. Night had not yet completely fallen by the lake, where the sky was still brushed with a fading smear of pink from the setting sun. But in the thick woods, fireflies twinkled and winked in the darkest spaces between the trees, and the stars already glittered brilliantly.

She stepped onto the trail, let herself be swallowed by the wooded dark.

Max was in a groove, at home in the darkness and halfway to the cabins when she smacked full force into a person nearly running the opposite way on the trail. It took all her willpower not to scream.

The other person grunted but didn't speak. Two strong hands gripped her shoulders, too tightly. Max felt hot breath against her face, the other face too close. The panic in her chest and veins was a wild animal.

Max struggled against the firm grip. She strained to see the person's face, but the darkness was too complete.

"What do you want?" Max wheezed.

The other person responded with a garble.

Slowly, Max's eyes adjusted and the liquid fear that swirled in her belly spread to her limbs and head, dizzying her. She gasped.

"*Chuck?*" she choked.

He clutched her more tightly, and Max's terror multiplied. It was a living thing, pulsing and throbbing through her entire body. Then the fear touched the dormant rage at her core, and her body swelled with fury.

"What do you *want?*" Max said again, this time with venom. "Let go."

Chuck mumbled. The sound was wet and swollen.

The fire inside Max dimmed. "Chuck?"

Another wet grumble.

Max yanked herself, hard, against Chuck's grip and he finally released her. She saw the shape of him in the darkness. His shoulders sagged. His breath hitched. But his eyes...his eyes shined in the soft starlight that filtered down through the thick trees. They were pleading.

"What happened to you?"

This time, Chuck didn't even try to reply.

"Say something."

Chuck shrugged and then he was gasping. No, not gasping. Max realized. *Crying.* Icy fear sliced through her, put her fire out cold.

"Chuck?" The gentleness in Max's voice almost masked her fear. Almost. "Talk to me."

"Mmmrrr," Chuck mumbled. "Hhnnggg."

"What's wrong with you?" Max said.

A new shadow loomed behind Chuck in the darkness, and Max gasped. The shadow engulfed him and pulled him away. A scream lodged in Max's throat, strangling her. She caught a glimpse of a uniform and she realized—not a shadow. It was one of the ranger men.

"Where are you taking him?"

The ranger's gleaming eyes met her own, but he didn't respond.

"What did you do to him?"

The man pressed his lips together and shook his

head. Chuck struggled in the man's arms, resisting the tight grip. Garbled noises and incoherent shrieks came out of his mouth. He sounded like a wild animal, and his wild eyes pleaded with Max.

Max lifted her chin and stepped backwards. Chuck's terrified wriggles amplified, but the man's grip was like steel.

Max met the ranger man's eyes in the starlight. Something deep inside assured her he was not to be feared. He wouldn't hurt her. She nodded. The man returned the gesture, a gentleman's bow. He retreated into the dark, a screeching Chuck in tow.

Chuck's unnatural shrieks—noises that sounded like a squealing pig on the way to the slaughterhouse—finally vanished into the dark and only the echo of them in her mind remained.

Adrenaline pumped through her veins. Her hands balled into fists and her feet rooted to the spot on the dirt trail. The sweet sharp smell of the forest pines lured her. She turned her head to the right and noticed, for the first time, an overgrown, unassuming foot path that veered off the trail and into the thick woods.

It wasn't a decision. Max's feet began walking on their own. She was deep into the forest before it truly occurred to her that she had left the main trail. A small voice inside told her to go back, to retrieve the drawing of Chuck, head back to the campfire, and join the other girls. But Something called to her. Her feet kept moving forward.

The trees were thick, the forest alive with cricket

song and twigs snapping with the bustling of nocturnal animals. Max knew these woods were home to animals worse than squirrels and raccoons, ones that preyed on girls. Animals that could smell a far distance. That would know she was alone.

She felt disconnected from her body, as though she was in a dream. Something urged her forward, a gentle tugging within. It wanted her to know.

"Know what?" Max whispered.

There was no answer. Just the sounds of snapping twigs and skittering feet; the lilting songs of the crickets and katydids and the soft, muffled padding of her own feet on the under-traveled path.

Max wasn't sure how long she had been walking. It could have been minutes or hours. All she knew was forward motion. Her head felt hazy. Just when Max thought maybe she would be walking the entire night, the trail emptied into a clearing, illuminated by the waning moon.

"What on *earth*?" Max whispered, horrified.

# PART TWO: BLOOD

# CHAPTER ELEVEN

The first horrible thing was the skulls. What could only be *human* skulls.

The clearing was a huge circle, and hundreds, if not thousands, of skulls lined its border.

Max laughed sharply, the sound too loud and jarring in the ghostly environment. The way the skulls lined the clearing reminded her of how her mother lined her garden with stones.

At the center of the enormous circle, there was an enormous pile of even more skulls. Narrow paths lined with additional skulls stretched from the pile to the circle's skull parameter, like spokes in a wheel. At the end of each tiny path, staked into the ground at the circle's edge, were huge crosses.

Max counted the tiny paths and crosses.

Thirteen.

"Thirteen cabins," Max whispered.

Light from the waning moon washed into the opening, illuminating the pale white bone. At the base of each cross, the ground was stained deep black.

Not black, she saw now. Deep, rust brown.

Blood.

Max reeled. Her heart raced. Her sense of time was disoriented. Camp Neverland wasn't safe, after all.

That's when Max realized that, scared as she was, fear wasn't the biggest emotion coursing through her body. There was something sharper and far more painful than terror.

Grief.

Camp Neverland was just another disappointment. The promise of friendship, of finally belonging, was merely a lure into a trap.

The camp brochure that had mysteriously arrived appealed to each one of her senses, seen and unseen. The camp promised reprieve. Artistic fulfillment.

Lies. All of it.

It had been bait, to get her here, to get her into this clearing.

They were going to kill her.

Not just kill her. Sacrifice her.

It had to be her, right? She was the only girl in Cabin 13 who had never been here before. And she was a virgin. Wasn't it always the virgin in these kinds of stories? Violet would know. It had felt so good to believe she belonged, even if only for a little while.

Yes, Max was sure she would be the sacrifice in Cabin 13. The sacrifice for what—*to whom*—she didn't know.

She needed to contact her mom. Go quietly back to Cabin 13, gather her things, and head out. Walk until she found a house, beg for help. She could call her mom from there.

Max cherished the fantasy, even though deep down she knew things never ended well for lone girls on remote highways running from hateful things in the woods.

Max breathed deeply, the sharp pine scent already tinged with the ache of nostalgia. The summer that was *almost* perfect.

Yes, Max thought. It was time. Her mind was made up. She spun on her heels, eager to leave the clearing behind.

Someone blocked her way back through the woods.

A scream lodged in her throat, panic filling her body and pushing against her skin.

# CHAPTER TWELVE

"Lost?"

It was Jules.

Max's heart hammered. "I..."

Jules' purple hair nearly glowed in the frosty moonlight. "I remember how I felt the first time I saw it," she said. "It's something else, right?"

Max swallowed. Her mouth was so dry. "What is this place?"

Jules crossed her arms and stepped back, a surveying stance. Her eyes roved affectionately over all the details of the clearing. "You remember the story Miss Flo told that first night?"

Max shook her head. That night seemed so long ago.

"The...snake woman?" she said, finally.

"This is where it happened," Jules said.

"That was just a...story," Max said. "The snake woman wasn't real. She couldn't be."

Jules cocked an eyebrow. "Why not?"

"There are so many." Max took in the skulls with new eyes.

"Each man deserved it." Jules' voice carried no malice, no anger. She was simply stating a fact.

"How do you know?"

"*Most* men deserve it."

Max thought of her dad. How she had felt when he left. How her mom had cried for weeks and tried to hide it, tried to be *strong* for Max. The look on her mom's face when she found out he was getting married again just two months later. Her mom had stopped crying after a while.

Did her father deserve this?

Max wasn't sure if he was a good man. He wasn't a *bad* one, either.

Max's eyes stuck on the dark stains at the base of the crosses.

"That blood doesn't seem so old," Max said.

Jules smirked. "Blood stains can last forever."

"Am I safe here, Jules?"

Jules' expression softened. "Haven't we made that clear enough?"

"This place doesn't exactly scream 'safe.'" Max gestured at the skulls and crosses and the whole eerie arrangement.

"We want you here," Jules said. "You belong with us."

Max's insides warmed. "Will I be killed?"

Jules looked genuinely shocked. "Killed?" she said. "*You*?"

Max nodded.

"*You* do not need to worry," Jules said.

"I ran into Chuck on the way here," Max said.

"Oh?"

"He didn't seem right."

"How so?"

"He was scared," she said. "It was like he couldn't speak. His voice was all...weird. I don't know." Max shuddered, remembering the strained, wet sounds that spewed from his throat. "It wasn't right."

"Max." Jules spoke with slow, patient tones. "Let's get back to the main grounds. We'll get your drawing. The girls are waiting for us back at the campfire. We need to hurry if we're going to make it before curfew."

The picture. The fire. The spell. All so far away. A feeling in the pit of her stomach told Max this was her last chance to go home.

"Maybe I should have my mom pick me up," Max said.

"Do you trust me?" Jules said.

Max searched Jules' eyes and found only earnestness and honesty. Max looked once again at the bizarre circle of skulls and blood-stained crosses. "This is wrong."

"But do you *trust* me?" Jules said. "And the others?"

Max inhaled shakily. ""I do. But this..." she said, gesturing at the frightening surroundings.

"I felt the same, my first time," Jules said.

"Why'd you stay?"

"Same reason *you* want to stay," Jules said. "Being here is like being home. Here, I've never been treated...I've never had to *defend* my right to exist. As me. You *belong* here with us, Max."

Despite reason, Max wanted to stay here with the girls who had embraced her without question. She didn't want to go back to microwaved dinners in front of the television and watch re-runs.

Max closed her eyes and breathed in the sweet sharp smell of pine, felt the whisper of the cool evening breeze against her cheeks. The wildness of this place lured her. Max sighed. "One thing I don't understand."

"What's that?"

"Why leave it?" Max looked again at the blood stains. "Why not tear it down? Bury the skulls? Put this place to rest. It just feels so..." Max shuddered.

"Alive?" Jules said. "That's why. Some places are sacred. Would you tear down Stone Henge? Put *it* to rest?"

"I'm not sure that's the same thing..."

"Close your eyes."

"What?"

"Close your eyes," Jules repeated.

"Why?"

"Humor me."

Max stared at Jules a long moment, a shiver in her

spine. Jules' eyes were steady and sane. Max nodded and lowered her eyelids.

"Take a deep breath," Jules said, gently.

Max inhaled. The cool night air tasted of residual sunlight and pine sap.

"Now, what do you feel?" Jules murmured.

Max cracked an eyelid to peek at Jules. "Huh?"

"Shhhh," Jules said. "Go with it. What do you *feel?*"

Max sighed and closed her eyes tightly. At first, she felt nothing but the cool kiss of night air. But then...

Her eyes popped open. "What *is* that?"

"It's okay," Jules said, softly. "Don't fight it."

Max closed her eyes again. And once again, she felt it.

It was a war cry in the pit of her belly, at the base of her spine. The ground beneath her feet hummed fiercely, a pulse spiked with adrenaline and fury. It vibrated with rage and vindication. The vibration traveled up her legs, electrified her body. The red-hot energy traveled up her spine and out the top of her head, so the crown of her scalp felt opened and buzzing.

Max was a tree, grounded and rooted into the earth's hot core. The earth's soil spoke to her, claimed her. This place was rage and fury, but it was also the fierce fire of love. And beneath that, an ancient ache. A yearning. The molten lava, the magma, the earth's lifeblood of this place filled her. Max was certain that if she opened her eyes, she'd be glowing.

Max smiled.

"See?" Jules said.

Max nodded.

"It's the heart of Camp Neverland," Jules said, softly. "We can no more destroy it than cut out our own hearts."

Max opened her eyes, slowly, luxuriantly, like a sleepy cat waking up. She examined her arms and hands in the moonlight, surprised to find that she wasn't glowing like an ember. "What does it want?" she said.

"What every woman wants," Jules said, smiling. "To be witnessed. To be loved. To belong."

Max nodded. Yes. That felt true.

"It *wants* you here," Jules said. "*We* want you here."

Max nodded.

Jules reached for her hand and Max took it. Jules' skin against her own was real, a contrast to the surreal, dreamlike experience from mere moments ago. She allowed Jules to lead her out of the clearing and back onto the foot path that led into the dark woods.


# CHAPTER THIRTEEN

It was satisfying to watch Chuck's face warp in the flames.

The paper curled, edges rippling bright orange, Chuck's face melting and distorting. All the rage and pain she had poured into the drawing vaporized with the rest of the paper.

Spell or not, it was indeed cathartic to watch him burn.

The five girls pressed their shoulders together at the campfire's edge, gripping mugs of cooled cocoa. They watched the drawing turn to ash and ember, small orange bits caught and carried away by the night breeze. They sparkled above the fire before they cooled, flashes of orange light fading and disappearing in the dark.

"Any words, Max?" Tanya said, pale hair glowing orange in the firelight.

Max wakened from her reverie. "Um, like what?"

"To seal the spell."

"Well...I'm not sure..."

"Close your eyes," Jules encouraged. "Feel what's in your heart. It'll be the right thing."

Max closed her eyes and found her body still vibrated with the heartbeat of the land. Crackling energy pulsed through her veins, a sensation like a lit sparkler. Max felt into her heart and Jules was right. She did find words there.

"Be gone." Max's voice was low, but clear. "You have no power over me."

Her eyes were still closed. The other girls pressed their bodies against her even more tightly. "Be gone," they said together, their four voices perfectly synchronized.

Then, a third and final time, all five of them repeated, "Be gone."

Max opened her eyes. The drawing of Chuck had completely disintegrated into pale white ash, much of which was caught by the summer breeze and carried off into the night. A sense of certainty, of finality, burned into her heart.

"It's done," she said.

"So mote it be," Jules murmured.

The other three nodded and spoke in unison: "So mote it be."

Max noticed that most of the other campers had begun the trek back to their cabins for the night. If the other campers thought the behavior of the girls from Cabin 13 was strange, they didn't show it.

"Shall we?" Tanya said.

"I need my goddess rest," Violet said, stretching her arms above her head and yawning.

The girls turned from the fire and headed toward the trailhead. Izzy hooked her arm into Max's.

"Epic first spell," Izzy said, her voice close to Max's ear in the dark. "Can't you feel it?"

The weirdest thing was, she could.

Izzy squeezed her arm. "I really am sorry about the mug."

"Don't be," Max said.

"You're part of our crew," Izzy said. "I'll start on it tomorrow."

Max squeezed Izzy back and savored what it was to belong.

# CHAPTER FOURTEEN

A cluster of laughing boys on the trail behind them burst through, breaking the group apart.

The boy in the front, who had severed the connection between Izzy and Max, laughed the loudest. His curly blonde hair fell across his eyes, which gleamed wickedly in the dark.

"What have we here?" he said.

Tanya crossed her arms over her chest, wraithlike hair glowing. "It's nearly curfew," she said. "Aren't you on the wrong side of camp?"

The boy grabbed a strand of Tanya's long hair and tugged. "Good little rule follower, eh?" He laughed. "Mind your business."

"We would," Jules said, "but you've made yourselves our business."

The five girls were surrounded.

"Leave us alone," Izzy said, "and we'll leave you alone."

"Hear that, boys?" the tall blonde boy said. "They think they're a threat."

The other boys laughed. One of them said, "Maybe we should see."

The curly haired boy stooped down nose to nose with Max. His breath was hot, an assault of curdled marshmallows, soured chocolate, and rank booze. "I heard redheads are wild," he said. "That true?"

Max leaned away from him, the back of her body pressed into the girls behind her. "You're drunk," she said.

The curly-headed boy jutted his lower lip into a mock pout. "Awww, boys, appears this one is no fun," He twirled one of Max's curls between sticky fingers.

Max's stomach churned with rage and fear.

Jules had been right, back in the clearing. Give boys some alcohol and a group of girls on a dark path in the woods, and they were all the same kind of animal.

The five girls linked hands. Max closed her eyes and found that her body still vibrated with the electricity from the heart of Camp Neverland. The earth pulsed against the soles of her feet. The life of Camp Neverland pulsed through their circle, thrumming through their linked hands, vibrating through their bodies. It burned through them, lit them up.

"What the..." The boy said.

Max cocked her head to one side.

The boys stumbled backward on the trail.

"Go," Max said.

But it wasn't her voice. It was the voice of the trees and the earth, the voice of lightning, the voice of rain, the voice of deer and bears and raccoons, the voice of wildness and blood. The voice of Mother Earth—and she was pissed.

Electricity passed among the girls, sparking through their linked hands and arms, lifting their hair with static.

The boys cowered on the trail, eyes wide.

The girls tipped their heads back and laughed, a sound of howling wolves and creeping insects and hissing snakes.

"*Go!*" They shrieked, voices one with the night, the land, the heart of Camp Neverland.

The boys took off running in the opposite direction on the trail, tripping over loose shoelaces as they went. They disappeared into the night.

When the girls finally let go of each other, the lightning that sparked through them slowly died down and fizzled out. It went back into the earth, dormant but aware.

The air still smelled of electricity. Their hair still floated around them, charged with static.

They walked back to Cabin 13 without speaking. Their bond had evolved beyond words.

Inside the cabin, they each changed into pajamas and crawled into their bunks. Tanya tugged at the pull string and plunged the cabin's interior into darkness.

But Max was still electrified with power. She still felt the earth's unquenchable thirst. Her throat ached with the rawness of it.

She clicked on her personal flashlight and pulled her sketchbook from her bag. She climbed into her sleeping bag and rolled onto her stomach, opening her sketchbook to a blank page.

And she drew.

# CHAPTER FIFTEEN

The next morning, the boy with the curly blonde hair was dead.

He was nailed to the big oak tree outside the mess hall. He hung upside down, flesh stretched and splayed to hold him up. What was left of his entrails dangled out of his opened stomach. The intestines too close to the ground had been devoured by animals. Blood pooled beneath him, bloody footprints from ravenous scavenging animals spread out in all directions.

Like the first boy, his body baked in the morning sun. The stink was unbearable. His curly blonde hair was gently tousled by the morning breeze, a sight that was eerily placid against the nightmarish scene.

The details were exact. She searched herself for guilt but found none. Her lower lip jutted out. It's not as though she had *actually* killed him. *She* hadn't been the one to nail him to the tree.

And anyway, the boy had deserved it.

Hadn't he?

A small crowd of gasping, murmuring campers had gathered in a half circle around the outside of the mess hall.

Miss Flo, tall and unshakable in a maroon track suit, cut through the crowd. Four men dressed in ranger garb followed silently behind.

Max's stomach did a somersault. A drawing wasn't proof of anything.

Max searched the gathered crowd of campers for

Chuck, but she didn't see him. She recalled the wet, garbled sound of his voice.

Miss Flo stopped at the front of the gathered crowd, while the men continued on toward the body. She pursed her lips.

"Campers, I understand your worry," Miss Flo said, her voice bright and full of authority. "Please, don't allow this incident to be cause for further alarm."

Miss Flo's presence had a soothing effect on the frantic energy of the gathered campers. The buzz of panicked chatter slowly settled.

Nothing about any of this followed any kind of official protocol, but this time, Max simply didn't care. It was clear by now Camp Neverland wielded its own justice.

"Breakfast awaits," Miss Flo continued, her seductive voice a tempting lure away from reason. "Go inside, eat, and when you're done, this nonsense will be cleaned up."

The group followed the rest of the campers into the mess hall, content to leave matters to the mercy of the camp's heart.

Max filled her tray with piles of steaming hot food. She and her cabinmates climbed onto the benches at their usual table. It was there Max felt the first pinpricks of guilt.

She wasn't ashamed of the drawing, but she did feel guilty for hiding it from her friends. They were clearly no stranger to magic.

Still, Max wasn't ready to divulge her greatest

secret.

Max dug into her food, the flavors bright and indulgent. She was ravenous, and she devoured every last bite.

# CHAPTER SIXTEEN

The following week passed without incident. Max hadn't seen Chuck since the encounter in the woods, and ever since the cord-cutting ceremony she hardly thought of him. Max settled into a rhythm.

The morning sunlight splashed through the cracks on the window shade onto Max's bunk and warmed her face. She smiled and cracked her eyes open, whispered, "Hello," to the sun. She stretched and yawned, then swiveled her feet onto the cool wooden floorboards. She padded into the bathroom to pee. When she pulled her pants down, bright red blood stained the inside of her underwear.

"Crap," she murmured.

"What is it?" Violet's voice called to her from the cabin's main area.

"My period," Max called back. "Tampons in my backpack."

She heard sounds of stirring in the cabin's main area, and then Violet appeared in the bathroom doorway. She tossed the tampon to Max, who caught it.

"Thanks," Max said.

Violet smiled sweetly then closed the thin bathroom door.

"New Moon tonight," Tanya called from the main room.

"Yeah, I know," Max replied.

Everyone in camp did. The whole camp was abuzz with anticipation over the upcoming New Moon ceremony—finally, the night of the mysterious Initiation had arrived.

Max finished up in the bathroom and wadded up her bloody underwear. She'd need to get a clean pair out of her duffle bag. She washed her hands, then opened the bathroom door.

"Pretty cool," Tanya said. She was still curled up inside her sleeping bag, pale hair a silvery nest.

Jules was cross legged on her bunk with her tarot deck, cards spread out before her on her sleeping bag. Violet was in her bunk, reading her worn copy of *Grimm's Fairy Tales*. Izzy, still tucked into her sleeping bag as well, stretched and yawned.

"What is?" Max said.

"Your cycle synced up with the moon," Tanya said. "Period with the New Moon is an omen of great power."

Max stopped in front of her bunk. Her sketchbook was not in her backpack where she had left it. It was on the middle of her mattress, opened to the gruesome drawing of the curly-haired boy.

Violet looked up from her book, eyes sheepish behind thick blue glasses. "It was an accident," she said.

Max nodded vigorously, cheeks burning. "It was, I swear! I didn't know for sure he would die."

Violet glanced at Tanya, who was now sitting up, face focused and intense.

"No...that's not..." Violet spoke carefully. "What I meant was, I wasn't trying to snoop in your bag. I was looking for your tampons, and when I saw, I thought, maybe, we should talk."

Max shoved her matted red curls away from her face, heartrate spiked. "Um, sure," Max said. "About?"

Tanya leaned forward. "Are you *okay*, Max?" she said.

"Okay?" Max's voice was a squeak. "Great. Never better."

"It's not your fault, you know." Violet's voice was gentle.

Jules didn't look up from her tarot spread, but she jutted out her lower lip. "We're always blaming ourselves," she said, "when boys behave badly."

"Well, it's just." Max snatched up the sketchbook and closed it, stuffed it quickly into her bag. She should have told them from the very beginning, but she'd been afraid.

"We don't blame you," Izzy said, stretching luxuriously again. "We've all...done things."

Max looked up, apprehensive. "Like what?"

Tanya said, "We know about your drawings."

Max sat down slowly in her wooden desk chair. "It isn't possible though, is it?" she said. "It can't be."

"You'd be surprised what's possible," Jules said,

pulling another card and flipping it over next to the others. "When you push a teenage girl to her limits."

"I didn't mean to upset you," Violet said. "We just thought it was time. We don't want you to feel alone."

Max hugged her knees into her chest and tried to slow her breathing. Something Tanya had said was bothering her. "But—how do you know?" Max said. "I haven't told anyone."

Tanya reached for the brush on her wicker nightstand and started to smooth out her pale hair. "We told you from the beginning," she said, "Camp Neverland is special."

"I never wanted them to die," Max said. "I didn't know."

"How could you have?" Violet said, closing her thick book.

"I guess I knew it *could* happen. Other things have..." Max chewed her lip. "But I've drawn lots of people dead. It's never gone this far."

Tanya smiled. "You've never been at Camp Neverland before."

"Am I...cursed?" Max avoided their eyes.

"Girl, please," Izzy said, stretching. "These boys deserve all that—and more."

"So why have them here at all?" Max said.

Jules finally looked up from her cards and raised an eyebrow. "We told you. We need them," she said. "Are you ready for the Initiation tonight?"

Max noted the abrupt subject change but was relieved to move on from the topic of her drawing. "I think so," she said.

"Nervous?" Violet said.

"Should I be?"

"No way," Izzy said. "It's the best night."

Tanya smiled from her perch on her bed, strands of silvery hair in her hand. "It will change your life," she murmured.

But Max's life was already changed.

# CHAPTER SEVENTEEN

The sky was washed in brilliant golds, deep crimsons, rich purples, soft pinks, and bursts of fiery orange. Max sat on her bunk, dressed in black jeans and her dad's *X-files* sweatshirt. She stared out the window screen, the soft evening breeze carrying sweet scents of honeysuckle and freshly mowed grass. It was a perfect summer evening, and Max wished to freeze time, bottle this moment, carry it with her forever.

The day had passed slowly, all the campers energized with speculation about the night's New Moon event, the much-anticipated Initiation. The return-campers remained tight-lipped, refusing to divulge any of the secrets, but clearly enjoying the build-up of suspense. Max had tried to work on her comic but was continually swept up in whispered anticipatory conversations with the other first-time campers.

Max observed the brilliance of the sunset, a tingle of excitement at the base of her spine.

She was interrupted by a soft poke in her ribs.

"How you doing?"

Max looked up to meet Jules' deep blue eyes. "Fine," she said. "Good."

"Ready?"

Max shrugged. "I think so," she said. "Am I?"

Jules winked. "Nice try." She mimed zipping her lips. "You won't get a word out of me."

"I wish I could walk with you all."

Violet hefted a big duffle bag and grinned. "Better this way," she said. "More exciting."

"And...I have to wear the blindfold?" Max chewed the inside of her lip.

Tanya pouted. "I know it seems weird," she said. "But it's tradition."

"Okay, but it's definitely in the clearing, right?"

The girls beamed but refused to indulge her curiosity.

"Remind me why it's called 'Initiation?'" Max said.

"We've already said too much," Izzy said, dark brown eyes sparkling.

"We have to head out," Tanya said, suddenly all business. When you hear the knock on your door, step outside and put your blindfold on. The man will hand you a rope and guide you to the site. Don't remove the blindfold until you're instructed."

Max shrugged. "Easy enough," she said. Weird enough, too, she thought.

The girls hugged Max. Their excitement was contagious. The tingle at the base of Max's spine grew and spread.

Jules was the last to hug her. When she pulled back, she nicked Max gently in the jaw with a knuckle and winked. "See you on the other side."

Max nodded, though she wasn't quite clear on the other side of *what*.

The four girls left, Cabin 13 suddenly empty and quiet. Max sat on her bunk and waited, watching the brilliant sunset erupt in a bold display of color outside the window. It was so beautiful it almost hurt. Max basked in it.

There was a loud rap on the door. Despite expecting it, Max still jumped at the sound. Her breath caught in her throat, her palms dampened.

Max walked to the door and opened it. The hinges squeaked. A man in a khaki ranger uniform stood there silently, holding a length of old, thick rope. He smiled toothlessly and gestured for her to come outside. She stepped onto the dusty front stoop and paused to retrieve her blindfold from her back pocket. Her eyes met his and he nodded, still without speaking. She lifted the blindfold to her eyes.

Max plunged into darkness. The cloth was rough against her skin. Max inhaled deeply, the dizzyingly sweet aromas of the fading forest day rich and vibrant. The man touched her shoulder, gently, then placed the frayed end of the thick rope against her palm.

Max took hold of it. When he tugged, she began to

walk.

# CHAPTER EIGHTEEN

Forest debris crunched beneath her feet. The ground softened as she allowed herself to be led onto less-traveled paths.

No light got through the blindfold. Without her vision, Max's other senses were heightened. Her nostrils filled with the sharp scent of pine and the rich smell of soil, the damp earthy aroma of decaying leaves and twigs. She heard the skittering feet of small creatures like squirrels, chipmunks, and raccoons darting for cover. The mingled whistles and caws of birds and crows, the flutter of startled wings.

Max breathed the cool twilight air slowly and deliberately, heart hammering against her ribs like a caged animal.

Then, abruptly, the man leading her stopped. Max did, too.

Max waited to remove her blindfold. If the walk had felt long, this wait seemed like forever. Max stood very still and listened to herself breathe. Listened to the man breathe.

Then, finally: the tip of the man's finger touched her temple, gently. His touch receded so quickly, Max thought perhaps she had imagined it. She waited, breathing, then felt another quick, gentle tap on the side of her head.

She reached up and removed the blindfold gingerly. She had expected it to be dark, but it wasn't.

Max blinked several times against the bright lights.

It took her eyes a moment to adjust, but then she realized what she was seeing.

She was on the narrow foot path to the skull clearing and it was lined by hundreds of flickering candles. She had expected this trail, but the candles were a nice surprise. The glimmering flames were a magical sight, there inside the deep woods. They beckoned Max.

The man stepped aside and indicated for Max to proceed without him.

Max walked forward on the candlelit trail. Her heart pounded, her palms damp with sweat. The candlelight cast an eerie glow against the darkening forest, making the tree shadows dance and warp grotesquely. The scene was beautiful and strange, surreal, and her feet carried her forward on the soft dirt path. It felt like a dream.

The earth vibrated against the soles of Max's feet, just as it had that night in the clearing—only it was stronger now. The forest and trees and earth hummed with a pulse.

Camp Neverland was alive.

Max smiled softly. She didn't know how she hadn't felt it the minute she's stepped foot here, the moment she'd left her mother's car. Maybe she had. Maybe she was only just aware of it now.

The earth sang against her feet. The forest roared the sweetest hum, a pulsating vibration. Max's blood thrummed in her veins, enlivened by the heartbeat of the land.

Max's footsteps became surer and more certain. Her legs carried her forward with purpose. She had the distinct sensation that she was walking, not just toward a mysterious camp activity in a creepy clearing, but toward her destiny. Her future.

Her whole body hummed and buzzed with the vibration of the forest. Max had never felt more ecstatic, more real, in her entire life. She finally stopped trying to resist the strange tingling sensation and succumbed to the waking dream.

Each deliberate step carried her forward on the path. The candles ended just ahead. Max's whole body hummed.

This was it.

A smile stretched across her face. She was eager. Ready.

She reached the end of the trail and stopped.

The clearing opened up before her like a mouth. The space was alive with candlelight, the skulls even more eerie than the first time she had seen them. Max's stomach twisted and her mouth went dry.

The heart of Camp Neverland.

It was inevitable. She had always been coming here. She had been the moment she had stepped foot on this land, the moment she'd left her mother's care. Max understood that now.

Max had expected to arrive in the clearing, but she hadn't truly grasped what she would find there.

Her head swam, dizzy from the land's vibration and the swirl of panic that thrummed in her veins. Suddenly, in her core, at the base of her spine, she understood. This was all very real.

Her choices were irrevocable.

And was too late to run.

# CHAPTER NINETEEN

Max clamped a hand over her mouth and stepped backward, bumping into the man. When she looked up at him, eyes wide, he returned her gaze silently. His stance was sturdy. He would not allow her to flee.

Max brushed tears off her cheeks and turned back around to face the clearing.

It looked just as it had the first night she had seen it, with piles of skulls at the center of the circle and small skull-lined paths that led outward from the pile to the edges of the circular clearing. Just like before: at the end of each small path were crosses.

Not like before: on each of the crosses, were boys.

Thirteen boys on thirteen crosses. One from each cabin.

Chuck was one of them. He opened his listless eyes. Then they met Max's and she saw it: a reckless, terrible plea.

Max looked away.

The boys were naked. Their hands and feet oozed blood where they had been punctured with nails.

The boys on the crosses weren't the only ones in attendance. Others knelt around the circle of skulls, naked, facing away from the center. Their faces looked strange, their eyes glazed as though entranced or hypnotized.

At the center of the circle, impaled on large stakes that protruded from the mound of skulls: the rotting bodies of the dead boys, mounted like grotesque scare crows.

There was a group of equally terrified-looking first-year campers, all girls, huddled together just to the right of Max, and she quickly joined them. Their eyes were also filled with tears and unspoken questions.

A twig snapped on the footpath and Max's head whipped around. A group of figures in black hooded cloaks emerged from the woods. She recognized Miss Flo's face at the front, then her cabinmates as well as all the other return-campers from other cabins.

Max took a shaky step toward them. "What is this?"

"Just as I've said, all along." Miss Flo smiled. Her head was hooded, but her skin rippled strangely in the shadows. "A safe space."

Max gestured toward the crosses and the bleeding boys. "Safe for whom?"

"Ah," Miss Flo said, hood wiggling around her face. "*That* is the question."

"This isn't right."

"If you're honest with yourself," Miss Flo said. "You'll know this is justice."

"What will you do to them?"

"Oh, my dear, not *me*." The hood around Miss Flo's head continued to writhe.

At that moment, as though they'd been waiting for this cue, some of the girls in black cloaks broke free from their position behind Miss Flo. They walked toward Max and the huddle of other first-year campers. When one of them stopped in front of Max, she realized it was Tanya, her pale hair barely visible beneath the hood. Each one of the other hooded figures who'd emerged stopped in front of each of the other campers.

Max met Tanya's eyes, but neither spoke. Instead, Tanya reached into her cloak. Max caught a glimpse of bare, pale skin. Tanya was naked beneath her garb. Max swallowed. Tanya procured a large knife from inside her cloak and offered it to Max.

Despite the cool night air, sweat dripped down the back of Max's neck. Heart pounding, she reached for the knife. She grasped it, though everything inside told her to refuse. To run.

This wasn't justice. The boys were unkind, but everyone deserved a chance at mercy. And Max was not a killer.

It was no common kitchen knife. The handle was bronze and set with jewels. It had an ancient feel. The blade strong and solid, sharpened to a fine tip.

Tanya returned with the other hooded girls back to

her position behind Miss Flo.

Max looked around at the other campers. Each girl had also received a ceremonial knife. Their faces reflected her own fear. They were all participants in a story much larger than themselves. It was far too late to change the ending.

Miss Flo stepped forward and removed her hood.

Underneath was not hair, but hundreds of tiny snakes. They writhed from her head, somehow attached to her, protruding from her scalp, yet also somehow separate and moving of their own volition.

Miss Flo allowed her entire cloak to open to reveal that her entire body was also made up of snakes.

A forked tongue darted from her mouth. Her hunger was palpable.

Hunger for blood. Hunger for revenge. Hunger for men.

"These boys have wronged you." This time, when Miss Flo spoke, it sounded like hundreds of hissing voices speaking in unison.

Max looked down at the knife in her hands. Then she looked at Chuck's drooping head, his body too weak to lift his neck and return her stare. The knife felt strange in her hands. Her whole body was covered in a thin layer of frightened sweat.

"He doesn't deserve to die." The words felt heavy in Max's mouth.

Miss Flo laughed in hundreds of voices. "My dear, they all deserve death."

Max looked down at the knife in her hands. "I don't

know if that's true." She looked at the girls next to her, the other first year campers with knives. Each of them brought here to meet a foe and enact their revenge. To satisfy Miss Flo's eternal thirst. "I'm not a killer."

"How do you think we found you?"

"*Found* me?" Max's voice sounded low and small.

"Did you think your invitation was an accident?" Miss Flo said. Then she gestured at Chuck. "Or his, for that matter?"

The brochure. It had been meant for her, after all. Max's throat swelled. It had also been meant for Chuck. All of this was on purpose. Orchestrated by...

"We are attracted to girls with gifts," Miss Flo said in a chorus of voices. "And gifted girls, well, they're often tormented."

Max swallowed. "It doesn't feel like a gift."

"It rarely does."

"I didn't mean to hurt anyone."

Miss Flo—*the snake woman*—laughed again. "Sweetheart," she said. "You can speak honestly. You are among *friendssss*."

But Max extended the knife, hilt forward. "I can't do it."

"My dear," Miss Flo purred. "You *have* killed before."

"Those weren't..." Max's palms sweat. "I didn't *kill* them."

"Did you not know what would happen?"

"They were just stupid drawings." Max's lower lip trembled. "I didn't mean it."

"Look inside yourself, Max." Miss Flo's hundreds of voices lilted. "You're not being truthful."

"You're wrong," Max said, tears welling up.

Jules stepped forward, along with Izzy and Violet, and they stood in a line next to Tanya.

"You can stay with us forever," Jules said.

"Forever?" Max said.

"We told you Camp Neverland is special," Violet said.

"Doesn't it feel good to belong?" Izzy said. "To be chosen?"

Max felt a tugging sensation on her insides, a deep sense of longing. The knife felt so solid and real in her hand. "My mom."

"She won't remember," Tanya said. "It's your life."

"We love you," Jules said. "Even the messy parts you like to hide. Especially those. You won't have to keep them secret, with us."

"Can you say that about anyone in your life back home?" Izzy said. "We *see* you. We can give you what they can't."

"We have given you that already," Violet said. "We want to be yours, every day, forever. Don't you feel it?"

Max nodded. The tears spilled freely down her cheeks. They were right. These girls, her *friends*, spoke to her heart. They had from the moment she had stepped foot on Camp Neverland's soil. "Aren't you homesick?" Max said.

"We're already home," Tanya said.

Max looked at the jeweled knife. She thought about

her mom, kind but distracted, always working, always tired. TV dinners on the couch, the ghostly light from the television illuminating their faces.

She considered her dad, his devotion to his new wife and children. Max was his firstborn, but she had become an afterthought.

She thought about school.

She'd been dreading the summer's end, the inevitable return to her life. Was it really possible that she could stay? Forever?

Max gripped the knife more firmly.

Her friends' eyes were so full of kindness and empathy, their hearts hers from day one. They were right. This was where she *belonged*. It could be her home forever and they would be her family.

Max raised her eyes to Chuck, nailed to the thirteenth cross at the edge of the circle. His chest heaved. His body was limp and tired, his head hung with exhaustion. She wanted to stay. But Chuck didn't deserve this.

"What if I don't..." Max said. "Does he have to..."

Tanya held steady eye contact with Max. "His blood is the price."

Her hands were hot and sweaty despite the cool night air. She looked around then, noticed that each of the other first-time campers were in similar clusters with their own cabinmates, each one in their own personal pilgrimage of choice.

Max swallowed. "I can't."

The group nodded in unison. "You *can*," Tanya said.

"We did," Jules offered.

Max looked to their faces, saw each one of them anew. Realized what they had sacrificed to be here. What they had gained.

"How long?" Max said.

"The years blur together," Tanya said. "In the best way. Time isn't the same, here."

"Ten earth years for me," Izzy said.

"Eight," Jules said.

"I'm the newest," Violet said. "Two years."

"But you all look so..." Max said.

"It's part of the magic," Tanya said. "We get to stay young forever."

"In exchange for..." Max scanned all the boys on the crosses.

"Their life has more meaning this way," Jules said.

"Think about it," Izzy said. "They're already dicks. How much do you think they'll change in ten, twenty years?"

"People change," Max said.

Izzy rolled her eyes. "That much?"

"We're saving them," Violet said softly. "And we're saving their victims. Present and future. Their deaths are noble. And they make this possible. They make *us* possible."

"But..." Max said.

"You either want to stay or you don't," Tanya said, "It has to be your choice. And your hand."

Max hefted the knife. She imagined what it would feel like to set it down. To turn around and go back the way she'd come on the foot path. To return to the cabin and pack her things. To walk into the main building, pick up the phone, call her mom, and say she was ready to come home.

Home.

As if where she lived had felt like such a place in a long time. Since her dad had left, at least. Maybe even before.

Home.

She scanned the faces of the girls who surrounded her, and she saw herself reflected back in their eyes. *They* saw *her.*

In her life back in New Jersey, Max was a shadow of herself. At Camp Neverland, she was real. Whole. Who she was deep inside stretched and breathed out in the open, in the Vermont sunshine. Existing and expressing were as natural here as the sweet honeysuckle and the sharp pine. These girls witnessed her. The forest comforted her. The land welcomed her.

Home.

Max gripped the jeweled hilt of the knife with sudden certainty. She nodded, then glanced around at the other clusters of cabinmates. She locked eyes with each new initiate in turn and saw in them what she felt in herself: resolve.

She walked forward and the other initiates followed, her resolve empowering them. Together they moved to the center of the circle, toward the mound of skulls and the kneeling boys. The impaled corpses extended toward the starry night sky, a morbid offering, bodies like warped and decaying gods.

Each girl took their place around the pile of skulls, facing outward. Max glared with determination at Chuck. His eyes widened.

The initiates stepped forward onto their own individual skull-lined path, each one leading to a boy on a cross.

Chuck trembled as she approached. His head and body sagged. He was naked and dirty, face tear stained. She stopped at his feet and looked up.

# CHAPTER TWENTY

Chuck's eyes were filled with tears and they implored her. He looked so human.

*Too late*, she thought, suddenly hot with rage. How often had she pleaded with him? And for what? The right to simply *exist*?

Existence should have been the baseline. The bare minimum. Max should have taken that right without asking because it had always been hers to claim. She saw that now. And she was done begging.

"It's your fault, you know," Max whispered. "*You* are not the victim here."

Chuck shook his head, hair matted with sweat and dirt. He emitted more garbled sounds from the back of his throat, still unable to speak after whatever they had done to him.

"Stop it," Max growled. "You sound ridiculous. And you know what? I don't care what you have to say."

Chuck emitted more frantic, warbled sounds.

"I said *shut up*," Max said. "You've had your time to talk. It's my turn, now."

Chuck began to cry. His chest heaved with sobs. His mouth warped into a grotesque frown; tendrils of shimmering saliva stretched from his lower lip toward his bare chest. Thick globs of snot poured from his nose.

Max cocked her head curiously and watched him shake with emotion. She knew he must be feeling afraid. He must want to live. How little compassion she felt for him. The more he cried, the uglier he became. Disgust filled her. Not because he was crying. She was no stranger to tears.

No.

It was because he had waited 'til *this* moment to reveal his humanity. Her tears had never stopped *him* before. And his tears now were too little too late. They fell on the soil beneath his feet, each drop an assault, a reminder that no amount of tears she had shed in the past had ever been enough to soften the hardened soil of his heart.

His tears watered the earth that pulsed beneath Max's feet, and her rage bloomed.

It was a curious thing, how easily the knife penetrated Chuck's heaving chest. How it slipped into his flesh, a knife in soft butter. Max had imagined it would be difficult. She had imagined she would hate it.

She did not.

The sensation was delicious. Waves of satisfaction rippled through her.

The flesh between his ribs was tender and soft, and the knife slid through the cage like a key. There was a just a beat, and then blood.

Oh, the *blood!*

It rushed out of the gaping wound in Chuck's chest and poured onto her, hot and slick. It coated her face and matted her thick hair. The bright metallic smell was intoxicating, and it wasn't enough. Too many layers separated her from the richness of the lifeforce that spilled out of Chuck. Max wanted to be one with it.

Max stripped out of her dad's X-files sweatshirt, slipped off her black jeans. She peeled off her bra and underwear and she was naked, bare feet on the soft wet soil. She stood in the shower of blood, thick and hot and rich against her skin. It gushed from Chuck's body onto hers, and she danced in it.

Her cabinmates tossed their black cloaks to the sopping red earth and joined her. His blood coated their bodies. They tipped their heads back and laughed at the dark moon, invisible but there all the same. The candlelight flickered, illuminating their red-drenched bodies. They opened their mouths and let his blood fill them with the penny-bright tang of copper, hot in the backs of their throats.

They writhed and twisted and laughed in his blood. Chuck's body convulsed. When the blood finally stopped, the girls looked at each other and howled, a sound that was primal and wild and free. The rest of the campers joined them in the primal sound, and they looked around to see twelve other clusters of naked, blood-soaked girls at the foot of their sacrifices.

Thirteen men approached the crosses. When one stopped in front of Max, he reached for her hand. She glanced at the other girls, who nodded encouragingly. She softened, and the man turned her wrist up toward the sky. He reached into his pocket and procured a needle, which he dipped into the gaping wound on Chuck's chest. He brought the needle to Max' wrist. His eyes were kind, yet apologetic.

"It's okay," Max whispered. "I'm ready."

He pushed the needle into Max's skin, and she gasped. The pain was sharp and bright. The process was painstaking without a mechanical instrument. The man went slowly, carefully, dipping the needle into Chuck's blood and poking it into Max's skin. Max closed her eyes and breathed into the pain, raw and burning yet surprisingly cathartic, almost euphoric.

At the height of agony, the man reached into his back pocket for a damp cloth and smoothed it across her skin. The cloth had a cooling, soothing effect on her fresh wound.

Max pulled her arm back to herself and surveyed the tattoo, the snake in the shape of a figure eight. Her eyes filled with tears, and she looked up to see the other girls were crying, too. It was official.

With the ceremonial tattoos finished, the Initiation was nearly complete. Miss Flo began to circle the group of remaining boys, naked and trembling around the pile of skulls at the center of the clearing.

"You have seen the fate of your brethren," Miss Flo said. "And while you have been spared because your hearts are not spoiled rotten, you are also not pure. You are accomplices to evil. You witnessed transgressions and stayed quiet."

The boys glanced at one another, faces tear stained, bodies trembling.

"However, I am not a woman without mercy," Miss Flo continued. "You may choose death," here she gestured toward the dead boys on the crosses, "or you may choose redemption."

The boys remained cowered on their knees, heads bowed and subservient.

"Excellent choice," Miss Flo cooed. "Then you will join my temple, worship at my feet, become my devotees. My silent protectors. I prefer men who don't speak."

She nodded almost imperceptibly, and the men approached the group of boys. Two men to each boy, one in front, and one behind.

"Stick out your tongues," she said.

Each boy extended the quivering muscles from their mouths.

Miss Flo nodded again.

The men in front of the boys leaned forward and down, mouths opened wide. Suddenly, their silence made sense—none of these men had tongues.

Max watched as each of the men took the boys'

tongues into their own mouths.

First, the clearing was filled with the sounds of singing crickets.

Then: awful sounds of choked, garbled screaming. The boys convulsed and the men behind them clamped their hands onto their shoulders, holding them in place.

It was a terrible thing, to watch someone sever another person's tongue with their own teeth. It wasn't as easy or clean as a cut with a knife would have been. But Max made herself watch, sensing it was her duty to witness.

When the men were finished, they spat the boys' tongues into the dirt. Some of the tongues wriggled on the ground, the nerves still activated and trained to resist. The forest filled with the sounds of choking, sobbing boys. Thick blood, black beneath the dark moon, shimmering in the candlelight, poured from their mouths. The men standing behind them released their shoulders and handed them cloths and gauze to staunch the bleeding. These men were living proof the boys would survive.

Jules turned to Max, the boys' distorted shrieks still echoing through the forest. "It's time."

She retrieved the knife from Chuck's chest. A final, thick glob of congealing blood oozed from the open wound.

Using the gilded knife, Jules cut into her palm. She handed the knife to Izzy, who did the same. Then Violet, and Tanya. And finally, Max. She dropped the knife to the ground.

Jules pressed a fingertip to the wound in her palm, and stepped in front of Max. She drew a line from the top of Max's forehead to the tip of her nose. Then she moved to the side. Each girl took a turn in front of Max, repeating the action, anointing her with their blood.

When they were finished, the five girls formed a circle and joined hands.

"Blood is blood," Jules said. "And now you are ours."

The girls closed their eyes. Max squeezed the hands in her own. The land pulsed beneath their feet, a heart beating with love. Energy surged through their linked hands, more powerful now that they were connected by blood. They stood like that for what felt like hours, their blood pulsing through their circle beneath the dark moon.

There was no external cue that the initiation was complete. They just simply knew. One by one, the clusters of girls all over the clearing released hands and began to leave the clearing. The legion of naked, bloodied girls walked, barefoot, along the footpath.

When they reached the main trail, Miss Flo led the way. Max and her cabinmates walked among the mass of girls, arms linked.

Soon, the trailhead opened up before them like a satisfied cat's yawn. A collective purr rippled through their bodies. They had arrived at the lake, which shimmered and sparkled beneath the wide expanse of stars.

The girls entered the water to bathe.

# EPILOGUE

Sixteen-year-old Jackie Whittaker sat in the passenger seat of her dad's pick-up. He smoked a cigarette—his latest in a seemingly endless chain—and blew the smoke out the open window just as he had the entire drive. A futile endeavor, as wind swirled the smoke right back into the truck's cab.

Jackie grimaced and tucked a strand of her short, straight brown hair behind her ear. She stared out the window. She gripped and twisted the worn pamphlet in her lap. Soon, she would arrive at camp, and she wouldn't have to smell his cigarette smoke all summer long.

After what seemed like an eternity but was really just a few hours, the truck finally turned onto the long dirt driveway, lined by pine trees. The majestic Vermont forest was both wild and welcoming, all at once. Jackie gripped the pamphlet more tightly.

Her dad pulled the truck to a stop in front of the main building. He snuffed out his cigarette in the ashtray he had wedged in the coin tray and brushed at his yellowed mustache. "I guess this is it," he said, voice low and gruff.

Jackie nodded. "I guess."

"I'm supposed to meet the lady inside," he said.

"Want to come in?"

"I'll wait out here."

Her dad nodded and coughed. "Be right back, then."

He disappeared inside the unassuming building. The screen door snapped shut behind him. Jackie sat in the truck and stared at the closed door, breath slow and even.

A rap on her window made her jump. She turned her head to the window and met the kind hazel eyes staring back at her.

"Oh! Sorry. Didn't mean to scare you."

Jackie opened the car door and lowered herself down from the truck's cab onto the dusty dirt lot. The girl who stood before her had wild, unruly red curls and a pale face with a spattering of freckles. She extended her hand, and Jackie took it.

"You must be Jackie. I'm Max," she said. "We've been expecting you. We're so happy to have you join us."

Lisa Quigley is a horror author and irreverent witch. She holds an MFA in Creative Writing from the University of California, Riverside's low-residency MFA program in Palm Desert. Her work has appeared in such places as *Unnerving Magazine*, *Journal of Alta California*, and *Automata Review*. She is the co-host of the award-winning horror fiction podcast Ladies of the Fright. *Hell's Bells* (2020) and *Camp Neverland* (2021) from Unnerving are her novellas. Her debut novel *The Forest* will be published in October 2021 by PMMP. Lisa lives in New Jersey with one handsome devil and two wild monsters. Find her at www.lisaquigley.net.

# REWIND OR DIE

01 – MIDNIGHT EXHIBIT ···············JONES, FRACASSI, MILLER
02 – INFESTED ·····················································CAROL GORE
03 – BENNY ROSE: THE CANNIBAL KING···········HAILEY PIPER
04 – CIRQUE BERSERK·······································JESSICA GUESS
05 – HAIRSPRAY AND SWITCHBLADES·················V. CASTRO
06 – SOLE SURVIVOR······························ZACHARY ASHFORD
07 – FOOD FRIGHT ·············································NICO BELL
08 – HELL'S BELLS···········································LISA QUIGLEY
09 – THE KELPING···································JAN STINCHCOMB
10 – TRAMPLED CROWN······························KIRBY KELLOGG
11 – DEAD AND BREAKFAST······················GARY BULLER
12 – BLOOD LAKE MONSTER····························RENEE MILLER
13 – THE CATCREEPER·······························KEVIN A. LEWIS
14 – ALL YOU NEED IS LOVE·····················MACKENZIE KIERA
15 – TALES FROM THE MEAT WAGON·······EDDIE GENEROUS
16 – HOOKER·································M. LOPES DA SILVA
17 – OFFSTAGE OFFERINGS····························PRIYA SRIDHAR
18 – DEAD EYES·················································EV KNIGHT
19 – DANCING ON THE EDGE OF A BLADE·······TODD RIGNEY
20 – MIDNIGHT EXHIBIT 2·····WARREN, MCHUGH, BURNETT
21 – THE GRIMHAVEN DISASTER············LEO X. ROBERTSON
22 – WHO WILL SAVE YOUR SOUL? ·····················JODY SMITH
23 – SOLE SURVIVOR 2·····························ZACHARY ASHFORD
24 – CHURCH·······················································RENEE MILLER
25 – SHE AIN'T PRETTY···································RENEE MILLER
26 – DESPERADO DINI·····································DUNKIE TANG
27 – CHOPPING SPREE·······························ANGELA SYLVAINE
28 – CITY OF THE CREEPS··········ERNIE KALTENBRUNNER JR.
29 – CAMP NEVERLAND·································LISA QUIGLEY
30 – TRANSMUTED············································EVE HARMS
31 – SKIN DEEP·················································RENEE MILLER

Made in the USA
Columbia, SC
19 September 2021

45776071R00074